BARRIE'S
BALLADS
&
MISCELLANEOUS
MUSINGS

ISBN 978-1-9993664-7-6

This edition published in 2020 by

The Lime Press
1 Lime Grove
Retford
DN22 7YH

BARRIE'S BALLADS

&

MISCELLANEOUS MUSINGS

BY

BARRIE PURNELL

ACKNOWLEDGEMENTS

Thanks to the trustees of my company
pension fund, whose efforts have
made it possible for me to live
comfortably without relying
on the meagre royalties
from this book.

Thanks to my two cats Cuddles and Tinker
For their unfailing loyalty and refusal
to comment adversely on my
literary shortcomings.

Thanks to Pat for everything.

STATEMENT

I offer no excuses for any of my actions
It matters not if I am wrong or right,
Every word is written for my own satisfaction
I am in control of everything I write.

I never wanted my verses to be holy psalms
They are not meant to be dissected or explored,
Their meaning isn't hidden but explicit
Not disguised within a dozen metaphors.

All the words I write have been discreetly hidden
Held safely in my mind ever since my youth,
No matter if they were sacred or forbidden
Only when written down had they any truth.

I am a compilation of many contradictions
A pessimist holding hands with hope,
Resisting attacks from opponents of tradition
I was in control of everything I wrote.

CONTENTS

MISCELLANEOUS MUSINGS   Page No

Dedicated to all those people
who think modern life isn't
all it's cracked up to be.

And

To Rosemary

BARRIE'S BALLADS

'Imagination was given to man
to compensate him for what he
is not; a sense of humour
to console him for
what he is.'

Francis Bacon

If ever a man was the pride of his clan
A man who stood out from the crowd,
A man who did his best when put to the test
Who with showmanship was over endowed,
Who'd perform for a fee with some sharp repartee
It was that Scottish magician MacMurdo McPhee.

His manner was gallant, a man of rare talent
He could do some impossible tricks,
He could balance on wires and juggle six rubber tires
While standing on two piles of bricks.
On a pier by the sea, or in a marquee
You'd find that Scottish magician MacMurdo McPhee.

He would practice for days his fans to amaze
He was famous throughout the land,
He'd swallow swords six feet long until they were gone,
And make doves appear out of his hand.
He lived in Dundee with a tame chimpanzee
That Scottish magician MacMurdo McPhee.

One trick on the stage that was all the rage
Was escaping like Harry Houdini,
He thought I could do that if I wasn't so fat
And it wasn't so easy to see me.
So he returned to Dundee for a nice cup of tea
Did that Scottish magician MacMurdo McPhee.

Having decided to try it he started to diet
And became incredibly thin,
He said I'll sure do that trick now I'm not so thick
I need something to hide myself in.
I need a box with a key and a door you can't see
Said that Scottish magician MacMurdo McPhee.

So to this end one month he did spend
Building his secret contraption,
In which he could hide and not be seen from outside
When he made his surreptitious extraction.
This just has to be the best trick for me
Thought that Scottish magician MacMurdo McPhee.

So he'd be shut in this box with multiple locks
And be dropped into a big water tank,
Then behind a large drape he would make his escape
Through a secret removable plank.
So no longer trainee but practiced escapee
Was that Scottish magician MacMurdo McPhee.

Without hesitation and much anticipation
He set out to perform his new trick,
Man, woman and child, all the people went wild
He had to beat the crowds back with a stick.
He performed in Newquay, Bournemouth and Torquay
Did that that Scottish magician MacMurdo McPhee.

But then a disaster befell this escape master
His best trick was also his last,
He failed to understand water makes wood expand
His secret plank becoming stuck fast.
He couldn't get free so he drowned don't you see
That poor Scottish magician MacMurdo McPhee.

Never again will we see a man like McPhee
Endowed with a talent so rare,
Addicted to magic his ending was tragic
It being a very public affair.
He died onstage so for me it was just meant to be
The death of Scottish magician MacMurdo McPhee.

His wife was from Aberdeen, she was grumpy and mean,
She said I'll give him the cheapest farewell,
So still locked in his contraption to her great satisfaction
She saved on his coffin as well.
So just outside of Dundee and almost for free,
They buried that Scottish magician MacMurdo McPhee.

SAM SMITH'S SEARCH FOR SHAPE
No pain without gain

Sam Smith looked at himself in the mirror
And wasn't happy with his reflection,
The shape of his stomach and chest
Both curved in the wrong direction.
My chest goes in, my stomach out
My body's upside-down,
If I want to get a girl, thought Sam
I have to swap them both around.

So Sam kitted himself out in Lycra,
And went to join the local gym,
And became quite disconcerted
By the sights confronting him.
Whichever way Sam looked
There were oiled up muscled limbs,
He could see even the women
Had bigger muscles than him.

Sam went to pay his subscription
The man said no fee would be due
If they could use his picture captioned,
'Don't let this happen to you!'
The floor of the gym was full of machines
The sight made Sam's heart sink,
The only one Sam recognised
Was the one dispensing drink.

Then he saw a piece of equipment
And thinking that's simple enough for me,
Looked for the operating instructions
But there were none that Sam could see.
He looked for someone who could help
And asked a track-suited wench,
How do I use this and what's it called?
She said, that sir is what we call a bench.

Undeterred Sam thought I must be brave
If I'm to get this body fit,
So he warily approached a treadmill
With more fear than he'd like to admit.
Gingerly Sam stepped onto the rubber belt
Gripping the handles tight,
And setting the speed to slow
Strode out with his left foot then his right.

Already visualizing his new physique
And thinking success was guaranteed,
With a plucky but unwarranted confidence
Sam increased the speed.
He started walking more quickly
Until he had to break into a run,
Then beginning to feel apprehensive
Sought to undo what he'd just done.

He reached for the speed controller,
That's what started the disaster,
In his hurry to slow it down
He'd turned the knob to faster.
Sam's feet moved inexorably backwards
Until he could no longer see his knees,
His face was red, his knuckles white
His body inclined at thirty degrees.

Sam's little legs could not respond
To his please speed up command,
And still hanging on tight to the handles
Sam ended up prone on treadmill's rubber band.
He felt a burning sensation where the belt
Contacted his downstairs private area,
He'd only felt this sort of pain before
With his crotch in the jaws of a terrier.

The friction between belt and Sam's Lycra
Overcame resistance of Sam's puny physique,
Dragging Sam's shorts to his ankles
Exposing the flesh of his vibrating cheeks.
He let go of the handles to grab hold of his shorts
A despairing almost fatal deed,
As the belt projected his body backwards
At a very surprising speed.

Sam shot across the floor of the Gym
Like a cannonball shot from a gun,
Mowing down Pilates performing ladies
Who were surprised by the sight of Sam's bum.
Sam slid on past where the gymnasts
Were putting their routines on trial,
The judge only gave Sam two for content
But gave him a nine for style.

Onwards sped Sam towards the Yoga class,
And without asking for permission,
Slid under some yummy mummy's tummies
Posed in the downward facing dog position.
Although the impact with the Pilates class
Had slowed Sam's speed across the floor,
He was still sliding much too quickly
Towards the closed gymnasium door.

Luckily for Sam it was automatic
And slid open as it sensed Sam's approach,
Surprising some young mothers in leotards
Who were just getting off of their coach.
A group of schoolchildren applauded
As Sam slid past them in an elegant glide,
Their teacher blushed red, shielding their eyes
From the sight of Sam's naked backside.

Sam finally came to rest in the car park,
Alongside the rack where cycles were left,
Before he could move a pensioner
Parked her bike in Sam's inter-gluteal cleft.
Extracting the wheel from his bottom
Sam was relieved he'd worn his athletic support,
The only thing preserving his modesty
As he pulled up the remains of his shorts.

Sam adjusted his tattered gym clothing
To cover all his previously private parts,
And made his way past some onlookers
Ignoring applause and ribald remarks.
He quickly hailed a passing taxi
And after appraising Sam of the cost
The driver asked, what's happened to you then?
Sam said, I had a fight with a treadmill and lost.

At home he looked at his ruined top
On which, 'Truth not lies' had been impressed,
Now only Truth remained the rest ripped off
By friction between the belt and Sam's vest.
Sam gave a wan smile as he realised
That due to his unplanned gym eviction,
Only the word Truth was left on his top
Proving indeed that *truth is stronger than friction!*

Sam realised he'd been overambitious
When he thought the treadmill was his friend,
And that men who get too big for their britches
Always find they're exposed in the end.
So Sam Smith decided to call it a day
On changing his shape to attract a wife,
No gain without pain proved right in Sam's case,
He had barely escaped with his life.

THE FESTIVE EXAMINATION
All's well that ends well

It dropped through the letterbox
With all the other Christmas mail,
I had no idea then of what
Its contents might entail.

It was a letter from the NHS
Asking if I would attend
For a simple routine check-up,
To which I could bring a friend.

Please read the leaflet the letter said
It will explain what you must do,
Before you attend the clinic
When we'll look inside of you.

I didn't like the leaflet's contents
It was more than I wanted to know,
Especially the diagrams which showed
Where the camera was to go.

It said take the enclosed medicine
The day before the test,
We need your insides sparkling clean
If we are to do our best.

I mixed the powder in some water
I had to drink it in one session
It tasted like diluted vomit,
With just the faintest hint of lemon.

Then I sat outside the lavatory
As the leaflet recommended,
Waiting for the potion to do the job
For which it was intended.

I sat there for about an hour
Then as I was about to give up,
Although potion was slow to start
Its final action was very abrupt.

I only just made it into the loo
This potion to be precise,
Was the laxative equivalent
Of a nuclear device.

The force of my defecation
Was like a jet engine on reheat,
Even though I held on very tight
I hovered one foot above the seat.

Then I had to repeat the process
And when action was complete,
I swear my bowels flipped into the future
Voiding food I'd yet to eat.

It did the job, I was empty
I was ready for my examination,
And I wasn't to eat another thing
As it would inhibit their observation.

Next day I sat waiting in the clinic
With a feeling of trepidation,
Wondering how even at this late stage
I could withdraw my participation.

I wondered what sort of camera they'd use
To push up my rectal passage,
Surely even a Kodak Brownie
Would do me serious damage.

Before I had time to think any more
About my size mismatch concern,
A nurse arrived who had a look
On the miserable side of stern.

Get undressed and put this on
She ordered passing me a gown,
It seemed a very odd garment
Front was open all the way down.

I didn't want to emerge like this
With all my bits out on display,
Then my nurse returned and said
Come out we haven't got all day.

As I shyly emerged she raised her eyes
In an expression of exasperation,
It's on back to front she said
Go and rectify the situation.

Doing as I was told I didn't think
The gown gave any better closure,
Because although my front was covered
My bum now had full exposure.

Follow me said nurse in a manner
Which gave no room for hesitation,
So trying to keep my back to the wall
I slithered sideways to my examination.

Lie on your side knees up, she said
Then started fiddling with her pens
I was hoping I wouldn't see the camera
Was a Canon with a wide-angle lens.

As I lay there backside out
Awaiting the coming penetration,
I was relieved to see a very large jar
Of medical lubrication.

Nurse said if you feel you need it
You can use some of this gas,
You bet I will I thought if you're going
To shove a Canon camera up my ass.

Doctor donned his rubber gloves
And showed me his camera instrument,
I was relieved to see the size of what
Was going to enter my fundament.

Here we go he said and with one quick shove
That greased up probe was in,
Doctor said nurse turn on the screen
And let the show begin.

He said you can look too if you want
And there upon the screen,
Were live pictures all in colour
Of my internal intestine.

It was odd to see my insides
Exposed for all to see,
Doctor said I'd cleaned up very well
To which I couldn't disagree.

Right up through my colon
This travelling camera went,
I'm surprised they didn't sell tickets
For this interesting event.

I was fascinated by the pictures
Before I saw them I didn't think
That my colon was corrugated
And was so very, very pink.

After surveying my internal landscape
Doctor said he was satisfied,
He said that wasn't too bad was it?
I said no............but I lied.

But overall it wasn't bad
They did it for a reason,
But it's not the way I'd chose to spend
The start of another festive season.

AIR'S A FUNNY THING
Words are lighter than air

Air's a very funny thing
You can't tell if it's fat or thin,
You cannot grasp it in your hand
It's very hard to understand.
It can be hot it can be cold
You don't know if it's young or old,
If you're cold it makes you colder still
A phenomenon they call wind chill,
If you're hot a breeze relief will bring,
Yes air's a very funny thing.

Air's got no back, it's got no front
You don't know if it's sharp or blunt,
It's colourless yet the sky is blue
It's odourless when it is new.
We need to breathe it to survive
Its oxygen keeps us alive.
You need air to speak and laugh and sing,
Yes air's a very funny thing.

There's no air at all in outer space
So for us it is a hostile place,
There's very little in the sea
Well not enough for you and me.
Air causes parachutes to float
And blows along the sailing boat,
It holds the glider up in flight
It's full of owls and bats at night.
I'm an engineer but haven't figured yet
How if air sucks up a jumbo jet
Then why doesn't it suck up everything?
Yes air's a very funny thing.

We call it wind when it is moving
If it's slow a breeze but it's confusing,
If it's fast a gale but I can't explain
Why if it goes round it's a hurricane.
All the air we breathe you'll understand
Has been used before, it's second hand.
Air does not discriminate
You breathe the same air as your mate,
The same air as the Queen and King,
Yes air's a very funny thing.

Is there anything as good as air?
It's always free it's always there,
It's very wide and very high
It obviously holds up the sky.
We all use it, plants renew it
What is best we can see through it.
Science says, and I don't doubt it,
None of us could live without it.
No there is nothing that can compare

With air, air, air, air, air, air, **AIR**.

THE TALE OF FREDDIE FAIRBURN
Fair's fair

You've heard of Freddie Fairburn
An accountant of renown,
He had the fairest hair
Of any fair headed man in town.

He was a mediocre man
Doing what normal people do,
He ate plain but nutritious fare
Like shepherd's pie and stew.

He only went out in fair weather
And kept out of the sun,
His skin was very fair you see
And was easily overdone.

Freddy wanted some excitement
A life in pastures new,
But he just could not think
Of anything different to do.

Then one day on his way to work
Feeling rather down,
He noticed that a travelling fair
Had set up in the town.

Freddy thought well here is
Something different I can do,
On my way back I'll visit the fair
And try out something new.

Taking a different homeward route
Freddie visited the fair
Amazed at all the fairground rides
That were on offer there.

There was a roller coaster
They had named Insanity,
Which moved itself around
At a very high velocity.

So Freddie Fairburn paid the fare
For this fairground ride,
And clambered up into the car
And strapped himself inside.

When the ride was started
It rose high into the sky
Turning upside-down and twisting
Seeming gravity to defy.

Then just when Freddie's lunchtime fare
Was about to be seen again,
It finished and Freddie Fairburn
Was back down on firm terrain.

Freddie Fairburn was still dizzy
Walking as if inebriated,
And was seen by a policeman
To whom the law is delegated.

He walked up behind our Freddie,
Alerting him with a cough,
Startling Freddie who swung round
And knocked his helmet off.

The policeman grabbed hold of Freddie
And said that's it my son,
I'm arresting you for that assault
You'll have to pay for what you've done.

Be fair officer said Freddie
I'm just dizzy from the fairground ride,
A likely story said the officer
You can tell your tale inside.

So Freddie Fairburn found himself
Locked in a cell overnight,
Bailed to appear in court when
He'd have to explain his fight.

His mood did not improve
When information he received
That the magistrate who'd hear his case
Was the dreaded Darius Deed.

Magistrate Deed was a man
Of strong religious conviction,
Retribution and not fair play
Was how he applied his jurisdiction.

He especially disliked those men
Who assaulted the police,
So was never very well disposed
To any breaches of the peace.

Freddie stood in the courtroom
Trembling and weak kneed,
Looking down, fat and perspiring
Was magistrate Darius Deed.

Well now, said Deed you seem to be
A man of sober disposition,
I am surprised to find you
In such an ignominious position.

I understand you had just left
That unsavoury travelling fair,
Let this be a lesson to you
Not to seek future pleasures there.

Although a first offence
My displeasure with you is clear,
You are fined two hundred pounds
And bound over for a year.

Fair's fair thought Freddie Fairburn
I think the magistrate was right,
I only got a fine and was
Locked up for a night.

As he bid the court farewell
He felt fairly relieved,
At the fairly lenient sentence
That he had just received.

As Freddie got out of the taxi
And paid the man his fare,
He pondered on what lessons
He had learnt from this affair.

His attempt at making his life
More exciting and titillating,
Ended with him feeling sick
And hyperventilating.

So next time he gets the urge
To stop living in an ordinary way,
Freddie Fairburn will just keep enjoying
Another ordinary day.

He realises his life is commonplace
But is without pretense,
He admires another's fairness
And values common sense.

Freddie does what most people do
And echoes what they say,
His television informs him
Of all the problems of the day.

He feels he is like most others,
Or at least nine out of ten,
He knows the whole country
Is run by mediocre men.

PENELOPE PRUDENCE POUND
You don't always get what you want

In Pavenham Hall in Penrith
Lived Penelope Prudence Pound,
She was just a little too short
And more than a little too round.
A woman of ample proportions
Five feet tall in stockinged feet,
Like a ship's figurehead her bosom
Preceded her down the street.

She had married a wealthy man
Much respected in the locality,
But Penelope Pound was a woman
Of great sensual sexuality.
She subjected her new husband
To twice nightly sexual exertions,
Which it's said sometimes included
Some unusual sexual perversions.

This put the heart of poor hubby
Under a very serious strain,
But his enjoyment was such that
He didn't want to complain.
There was no way he could stand the pace
That's the honest truth,
He just wasn't as young and virile
As he had been in his youth.

Fate intervened during one night
Of these sexual gymnastics,
Their antics unbalanced a bookcase
Stuffed full of leather bound classics.
The bookcase toppled over
Hitting poor hubby right on the head,
He had been classically trained you know
But now he was classically dead.

Penelope Pound did not take long
To leave her grief behind,
She was a woman with needs
And always had sex on her mind.
She wanted another partner
Yes she wanted another mate,
But she was out of practice at courting
And too shy to go out on a date.

So she joined an internet dating site
With a typically bold description,
'A mature woman with needs,
And a profile that's somewhat Egyptian,
Looking for a virile young man
Who is handsome with stamina to spare,
With an adventurous nature
And preferably all his own hair.'

Many potential suitors replied
But none who could replace,
The man who she had married
And who died with a smile on his face.
They were all a little too butch
Or just a little too camp,
And none measured up to the needs
Of our voracious vamp.

Then one day she met a man by chance
While out walking her dog in the park,
He seemed rather simple at first
But was tall and handsomely dark.
He was dressed all in red
With pointed shoes and a red felt bobble hat,
But there was just something about him
That made her stop and chat.

She vowed that this was a man
She just had to possess,
So the next day for their meeting
She wore her most provocative dress.
She stopped and engaged him
In polite conversation,
Asking about his job and his
Unusual red clothes combination.

He said I'm one of Santa's helpers
And I am here for just one reason,
I am only here in human form
During this Christmas season.
I'm here to make all humans happy
But if I am to stay
I must keep my pointy hat on
Both at night and in the day.

I am here to help fulfill
All your Christmassy desires,
Like fir trees with flashing lights on
And carol singing choirs.
I can do anything you want, he said
As long as good deeds form a part,
He could do me a good deed, thought Penelope
But I'll have to get him home for a start.

It wasn't long before she had lured him
Back to Pavenham Hall,
Where she found out to her surprise
He knew nothing about sex at all.
This was a man who she could teach
All of her sexual skills,
Educate him in all her perversions,
Including the one with the daffodils.

The poor man, he was so naive
He had truly no realisation,
Her predilections weren't normal
For the rest of the population.
Penelope Pound was as happy
As she had ever been in bed
Except that she couldn't stop this man
From dressing all in red.

Even when he went to bed
His bobble hat he wore,
One night after two bottles of Beaujolais
While he was sitting on the floor,
She grabbed his hat but he stopped her
Saying please, please don't do that,
You will find I am not the same man at all
If you relieve me of my hat.

But Penelope Pound was a woman
Who would never be denied,
She grabbed his hat and her lover
Just sat there mortified.
Then she wouldn't have believed it
If she hadn't seen it for herself,
He got smaller and ever smaller
He had turned in to an elf.

He said I warned you what would happen
But you wouldn't accept my explanation,
Now there is no way you can reverse
My transmogrification.
With that he slipped under the door
And in an instant he was gone,
All that was left was his red felt hat
With the bright red bobble on.

Penelope Pound was sad
She had lost her very best lover,
She just hadn't the heart to start again
And search for yet another.
So she turned to religion
And following her conversion,
She joined a group of celibate nuns
Of the holy order Cistercian.

We should all learn the lesson
From Penelope Prudence Pound
If your lover tells you not to it's best not to,
That is what she found.
He could be a pauper or a poet
An elf or an aristocrat,
You just don't know what you are going to get
When a man takes off his hat.

Sam was a burglar by trade
Ken was his best comrade
Known by the thieves in London as Keyhole Ken,
They worked as a team
And were awfully keen
They were both really hard working men.

They burgled houses in Harrow
And bungalows in Hounslow,
Which houses they burgled were all Sam's decision,
In Lewisham and Lambeth
In Waltham and Wandsworth
Ken opened locked doors with unerring precision.

Sam rarely gave a thought
About getting caught
But it was inevitable it would happen one day,
And as he stood in the dock
Looking up at the clock
Sam heard the judge asking what he had to say.

Sam said I don't mean to suggest
Of all men I'm the best
But I'm not really all bad just the same,
Though you speak of me ill
My work takes lots of skill
I can tell you, burglars ain't all the same.

We made a good living
And had no misgiving
About stealing goods that weren't strictly ours,
We targeted snobs
On most of our jobs
And we worked very unsociable hours.

Avoiding the Fuzz
Was what gave us the buzz
We weren't cut out to work nine to five,
We knew there'd come a time
When we'd pay for our crimes
But we took those risks just to survive.

As regards those we robs
They don't have real jobs
Exploiting others was how their wealth was made,
If it was me I'm believing
You'd call it thieving,
But these guys they put it all down to trade.

So I think its fine
To say what's theirs is mine
I work just as hard as they do to get it,
They take real pains
To protect their ill-gotten gains
And for my skill I get not one bit of credit.

But listen tell you I shall
About job me and my pal
Undertook inside a bankers large mansion,
We knew he had a big stash
Of jewelry and cash
You can see sir what was the attraction.

Inside information
Gave us safe's location
The job should've been easy if we were smart,
But as you can see
As your looking at me
The job went wrong right from the start.

No one heard us arrive
As we crept up the drive
Ken opened the locked kitchen door in an instant,
We mounted the stairs
Heard the banker saying his prayers
Safe was on the landing which was convenient.

The banker started to snore
So loud it vibrated the floor
There was no way he'd hear our criminal exertions,
But there was no lock to pick
This safe worked by 'lectric
There was no hole for normal key insertion.

We didn't have combination
And in this situation
We would have to chisel our way in from the back,
We put our wedge in at the top
Then came to a stop
Footsteps in the hall stopped us in our track.

A young woman appeared,
She looked a bit weird
Ken said looks like she's walking around still asleep,
So we crouched in the corner
So as not to warn her
And kept real quiet, didn't dare utter a peep.

She seemed to be gliding
Towards where we were hiding
And Ken wanted to put her out cold with his stick,
But force isn't my style
So I said no, wait a while
We'll just see what route she will pick.

She looked kind of strange
Her expression didn't change
I thought for sure that she must be sleep walking,
It gave us a chill
It was hard to keep still
I just hoped she hadn't heard us talking.

She came on up the stairs,
Ken and I said our prayers
When she came straight to where we were hiding,
Then bending down
She turned the safe handle round
As she opened the door I saw she was smiling.

We never thought me and Ken
The safe would be open
We assumed it was locked that was our big mistake,
She opened safe door wide
And reached her hand inside
When it came out we knew she was awake.

In her hand was a gun
We had nowhere to run
That long steel barrel pointing straight at us two,
She opened her mouth to shout
Ken leapt up to give her a clout
With a bang the gun fired and one bullet flew.

It hit Ken in the head
I knew straightway he was dead
It was his impetuous nature that was to blame,
Me I stayed on my knees
And said lady please
Don't shoot me us burglars aren't all the same.

Soon there came a crowd
All shouting out loud,
No use running they'd caught me fair and square,
When the police came
And took down my name
I knew this was going to be a serious affair.

I can only ask for your pity
Although I know I'm guilty
I'm a man of paradox and contradiction,
Despite my profession
I refrained from aggression
My peaceful nature led to my conviction.

That judge is how
I came to stand before you now,
Judge looked down at me and said he understood
About my situation
And plea of mitigation
But I'd have to pay 'cause my crimes were not good.

For my burglary career
He gave me fifteen years,
He said I hope this is a lesson crime does not pay,
You'll have time to contemplate
What led you to this fate
The officer of the court then led me away.

Now I'm spending my time
Putting my story in rhyme
To warn those of you tempted to stray,
That robbing and stealing
And stolen goods dealing
Don't look so good from where I'm sitting today.

I look out as the rain
Runs down the barred windowpane
Far from all of my family and friends,
All you who seek to deceive
All you robbers and thieves
Just remember this is how it all ends.

So if you're kind hearted
Just don't get started
You should pick a more honest occupation,
Stay home with your wife
Live a nice boring life
Then you won't find yourself in my situation.

THE PRATTS
All good things come to an end

The Pratt family looked on anxiously
As dad said finances were feeling the strain,
There was mum, dad, Emma and Percy
And it was holiday time again.

Flying to Miami is where they'd planned to be
A bit posher than a Benidorm beach,
But despite saving every penny
Miami was out of their reach.

Dad explained their plight that cash was tight
It would have to be a staycation,
But don't worry I'll make everything right
Your dad's planned an exciting vacation.

I had to choose so we're going on a cruise
This improved the Pratt family's moral,
That is until Dad said their time afloat
Was on the Chesterfield canal.

Giving neighbours their cat the family Pratt
With some reluctance and trepidation,
Boarded their narrow boat The Spritely Sprat
Docked in the Staveley Town Basin.

Pratt appeared unsure thought it a bit premature
When boat owner handed over command,
It seemed much bigger than in the brochure
When you were floating and not on dry land.

Boatman said be polite always pass on the right
And keep your speed set to slow,
Keep away from the banks and tie your ropes tight
That's all that you need to know.

Dad Pratt took command with wheel in his hand
He set off steering away from the banks,
Thinking this wasn't as easy as he had planned
He gave the boatman a quick wave of thanks.

He was still unclear about boat's steering gear
Which way to turn wheel to go left or right,
He moved down the canal like a drunk gondolier
Couldn't go straight, try as he might.

Pratt's face showed dismay as he zig-zagged on his way
As if trying to avoid a U-boat attack,
He cheered up a bit when he heard his kids say
Don't worry dad you'll soon get the knack.

Pratt had just put things right when he got a fright
Another boat was approaching head on,
Their skipper was obviously up for a fight
Shouting to Pratt he was the one in the wrong.

Pratt remembered the guide he was on the wrong side
A move to the left had to be his decision,
Jamming wheel hard over with full force applied
He narrowly avoided a head on collision.

Due to Pratt's distraction with avoiding action
He was now exceeding speed limit allowed,
And the size of their bow wave dimension
Attracted surfers from within watching crowd.

As through the water they churned their wash overturned
Two dinghies which then promptly sank,
A water-skier was hanging onto the stern
Two fishermen drowned as they stood on the bank.

Realising his mistake Pratt shouted, where's ruddy brake?
Demonstrating his lack of boating prowess,
He desperately looked for some action to take
As he sought excessive speed to address.

God have mercy, shouted Emma and Percy
Quickly pushing gear lever to reverse,
Thinking this might be the end of their journey
Pratt let out an involuntary curse.

Pratt's obvious fright caused much delight
To other more experienced sailors,
He thought that they were a tad impolite
Especially when they used a loud-hailer.

Pratt wanted to get clear and to disappear
So put boat into slow forward motion,
Donning his captain's cap and grabbing a beer
He was Columbus about to conquer an ocean.

After speed reduction Pratt saw an obstruction
A set of locks now stood in their way,
Pratt approached them with extreme caution
He knew for any damage he'd have to pay.

Lock entrance was awkward he crept boat forward
They only had inches to spare,
He tied the bow tight to the bollard
And offered up a mariner's prayer.

Pratt turned himself about saying let water out
And the water level it started to drop,
When only stern went down, he let out a shout
Asking wife water removal to stop.

With the prow tied up still, boat was sailing uphill
Although he'd followed boatman's instruction,
And tied the boat up with consummate skill
How had it led to this apparent malfunction?

Pratts knot tightly tied had bow descending denied
So boat was now held at sixty degrees,
The stern was sinking with Pratt still inside
He was in water right up to his knees.

Off hatch cover flew and water poured through
And flooded the engine and cabin,
The family said, dad this is all down to you,
This was worse than they could have imagined.

Pratt's observation of boats partial rotation
Showed abandoning ship was all he could do,
And acting now in some desperation
Onto the bank all their belongings he threw.

Our landlubber dope then just cut the rope
Boat fell back into the canal with a crash,
Pratt let out a yell then abandoned all hope
As boat promptly sank with hardly a splash.

Well that's ruddy that, holiday's cancelled said Pratt
It's been a disaster I'll have to admit,
Saying, I hate boats he stamped on his hat
Pratt knew he had lost his ruddy deposit.

I'm no longer a supporter of messing about on the water
It's just not a holiday suitable for us,
Then said to his wife, son and daughter
We'll finish this journey by bus.

In Lincolnshire where the land is flat
And the skies are big and blue,
Where people get a thrill at the sight of a hill
They can tell you a tale or two.

Of Freddy Fast who lived up to his name
He was a man addicted to speed,
He lived his life in the fast lane
He was one of a dying breed.

Freddy was even born in a hurry
He was three weeks premature,
He was born in the back of a Cadillac
Going at sixty miles an hour.

If this traumatized our young hero
It's impossible to know,
But some do say it's what gave Freddy
His hatred of going slow.

When Freddy was only five years old
He frequently could be seen,
Racing hard around his parents yard
In his peddle powered machine.

One day he peddled his little car
To the top of Wold Top hill,
Where Newton's law of gravity
Would test his driving skill.

Freddy's feet were soon rotating
At a speed he'd never seen before,
The slope had met his need for speed
And Freddy wanted more.

But he'd given no thought of what to do
When the hill came to an end,
And unfortunately for Freddy Fast
It stopped with a right angle bend.

At the bottom the car just went straight on
Hit the kerb and then took flight,
Freddy said a prayer as he flew through the air
Shut his eyes and just held tight.

The car cleared a ditch landing in a field
Behind a high stone wall,
Where luckily for young Freddy
A large fresh cow pat broke his fall.

Freddy's mum, looking through her window,
Thought, what on earth is that?
It was her confused and bruised son Freddy
Wearing a cow pat for a hat.

As a young man Freddy joined
A famous cycle racing team,
Someone at last paid him to go fast
That had always been Freddy's dream.

And as was his style he led the pack
Onto a very dangerous descent,
Then with one bad decision he had a collision
And over the bars he went.

Sadly this accident ended
Freddy's racing participation,
It was a suicide of a downhill ride
That put him in this serious situation.

When Freddy crashed down on the road
He had broken almost every bone,
To save on space they packed him up in a case
To send poor Freddy home.

As soon as Freddy had recovered
He looked for new ways to go fast,
He was more stupid than he was before
He didn't learn anything from the past.

He bought himself a powerful motorbike
And took it to the track,
In Freddy's world you just looked forward
He saw no sense in looking back.

Freddy's races only had two outcomes
He either won it or he crashed,
He would never choose any race to loose,
Because he liked the winner's cash.

One rainy day at Cadwell Park
Freddy's run of luck ran out,
The way he was running he had it coming
Of that there was no doubt.

He parted company with his motorbike
And that was the end of Freddy's race,
But when they picked his lifeless body up
There was still a smile upon his face.

He became a legend and he reveled
In the fame and loved the glory,
You couldn't pretend there'd be any other end
To the Freddy Fast life story.

On Freddy's final ride to the churchyard
He could no longer speed or misbehave,
And two flying birds and these few words
Were carved into the headstone on his grave.

Here lies a man whose talent for speed
Took him to the very top,
He lived life in the fast lane
But just didn't know when to stop.

WILLY WALTON THE WRITER
The pen is mightier than the sword

Willy Walton was a problem
To his parents and his school,
He just did not want to study
And preferred to play the fool.

He fell foul of all the teachers
And was always in detention,
They found they could not retain
Willy's full attention.

Except for the English teacher
Who seemed to have the knack
Of getting through to Willy
And keeping his mind on track.

She found Willy wrote very neatly
And his vocabulary was wide
And with homework that she gave him
She was very satisfied.

Willy's one and only passion
Was for the written word,
He didn't understand arithmetic
And thought chemistry absurd.

Words were what Willy thought of
Each day and every night,
He was never really happy
Unless he had something to write.

The school couldn't stop him writing
On the blackboards and the walls,
He even wrote on the equipment
In their gymnastic halls.

His verses detailed teacher's failings
And unfortunate afflictions,
And on the lavatory walls
Their sexual predilections.

In an effort to stop Willy
Indulging in his passion
They tied his hands behind him
In an arrested convict's fashion.

But when graffiti then appeared
On the school wall facing south,
They found Willy still writing
With the pen held in his mouth.

Willy's parents were at their wits end
With their errant son,
He could not do his algebra
And could barely count past one.

But he could write a description
Of any given situation,
With correctly indented paragraphs
And perfect punctuation.

What job can you do they said
If you can't even count to ten.
Whenever you count you get to three
Then have to start again.

There is no job that doesn't require
Some numerical application,
Except perhaps a minister
In Department of Education.

Then his teacher said he could become
A proof reading specialist,
Reading others writing, correcting
Mistakes that they had missed.

This seemed a good way out
Of a very difficult situation,
Willy got a job proof reading
For a publishing organization.

They sent Willy his first book to read
And he set to with zest,
He finished it within a day
And publishers were impressed.

Joy disappeared when they discovered
One detracting factor,
Young Willy had written and inserted
One new unwanted chapter.

Not only inserting a new chapter
What was even worse,
The chapter he had written
Was in perfect metered verse.

Why did you add that chapter?
The publisher enquired,
That was not in your remit
And was definitely not required.

Well said Willy, I read the book
And being a creative chap
I added in the chapter because
I believed the book was crap.

So that was the end of poor Willy's
Proof reading career,
And his writing withdrawal symptoms
Soon became severe.

He started going out secretly
Each and every night,
Looking for some surfaces
Upon which he could write.

He wrote upon shop windows,
With his black enamel spray,
On the local underpasses
And bridge over motorway.

Before long Willy's verses
Appeared upon Facebook pages,
His work was being talked about
By people of all ages.

His whimsical words of wisdom
Soon reached the TV news,
Literary critics were being canvased
For their considered views.

Some said he was a genius
Some said he was a fraud,
The local council cleaning squad
Just wished he'd move abroad.

On the internet his identity
Was the cause of much speculation,
And many wondered just what was
This secret poet's motivation.

His anonymity only served
To increase the interest in his verses,
Despite them often being libelous
And interspersed with curses.

Eventually Willy was unmasked,
Caught in his hometown square,
Painting rude verses on the backside
Of the statue of the mayor.

Arrested by the coppers
He was let off with a caution,
But they gave him a night-time curfew
Just as a precaution.

Then Willy's previous employers
A publisher of note,
Offered him a job and said
They'd publish everything he wrote.

Soon his books of perverse poetry
Were on every bookshop shelf,
And Willy became a literary
Celebrity himself.

He became prof. of poetry at Plymouth
And was listed in De Brett,
And then the monarchy appointed him
As poet laureate.

But his first effort as the laureate
Was not a great success,
This verse, for Prince Philips 90th,
Palace tried hard to suppress.

'Prince Philip has reached 90
And walks behind her Maj,
Insulting all those coloured folk
Who once lived in the Raj.'

'He's insulted both his subjects
The bishops and their God,
But no one cares because they know
He's a mischievous old sod.'

So from university and laureate
Willy was dismissed,
He fast fell out of favour
And became a calligraphist.

But then another unexpected
Opportunity arrived,
And the world of calligraphy
Of Willy was deprived.

Her Maj sent her representative
To ask on her behalf,
If he would come and work for her
Just to make old Philip laugh.

She said One must try to keep
Philips need for humour in control,
He finds society's PC demands
Are a noose around his soul.

So that's how Willy became the only
'By Royal Appointment' bard,
And can often now be seen
Strolling across the palace yard.

Now he uses his writing talent
By spending all his time
Keeping Maj and Philip laughing
At his very non PC rhymes.

DANGEROUS DAN McGAN
Look before you leap

In a northern town on a wasteland site
Was born a boy called Daniel Mcgan,
His mum and dad weren't very bright
They all lived in a caravan.

Dan never had any real ambition
He could write and almost read,
All his teachers had a suspicion
That was about all Dan would need.

Dan was forever playing the fool
Always up for a dangerous game,
For every prank that was played in school
Dan ended up getting the blame.

Leaving school he was under pressure
To answer an advert that he'd seen,
For young men with a sense of adventure
To act as extras on the movie screen.

He was one of those chosen by audition
Dan was excited at being selected,
He turned up with some apprehension
But his inexperience wasn't detected.

The first scene involved a stunt man
Leaping out of a fast moving car,
I could do that routine, thought Dan
Ignoring the man's prominent scar.

He started to absorb stunt man's knowledge
He was a natural he had no fear,
His stupidity was an added advantage
Dan had found his ideal career.

After an accident prone beginning
He played stand in for numerous stars,
Jumping off the rooves of tall buildings
And crashing exotic cars.

Dan's stunts were done by very few
He'd dive into water fast flowing and deep,
Paddle over waterfalls in a flimsy canoe
Ski down slopes incredibly steep.

There was no stunt Dan wouldn't do for money
Doing everything with panache and élan,
He became well known in the industry
They called him Dangerous Dan Mcgan.

He valued his reputation for being the best
For completing every stunt that he tried,
His strength was his physical prowess
His weakness his professional pride.

Being pushed off the Eiffel Tower was quite tricky
He was thrown from an aircraft by Jean-Claude Van Damme,
Knocked off a roof by Stallone playing Rocky
And died spectacularly in Good Morning Vietnam.

With the coming of virtual reality
Many stunt men were being retired,
Dan needed all of his stunting ability
For the increased risks that they required.

One day when Dan heard the phone ringing
It was a film director very well known,
He told Dan the stunt he was proposing
Dan was pale when he got off the phone.

It seemed like an invitation to suicide,
A stunt everyone else had refused,
But he decided, whatever he felt inside
Of cowardice he could not be accused.

The stunt the director had explained
Involved freefalling from high in the air,
Then parachuting onto an aero plane
Which sounded a very dangerous affair.

Then the plane's undercarriage he'd grab
While it flew alongside a fast driverless train
He'd drop onto its roof and run along to the cab,
Dan thought whoever does this is insane.

The train would be stopped when he could see
A wrecked bridge over a very deep canyon,
Impossible thought Dan but then saw the fee
For this one stunt they'd pay him a million.

After all of the risks he'd had time to digest
Dan said he'd do it, but still wasn't sure how,
So he trained until he was at his physical best
He'd never refused and wouldn't start now.

The day came, though calm his heart was racing
He strapped on his chute and was ready to fly,
With a deep breath he jumped out and was falling
His chute opened he drifted down through the sky.

He landed quite softly on the aero plane wing
Then worked his way under, it was touch and go,
Until onto the plane's wheels he was hanging
Gazing down at the train far below.

Dan was starting to feel the strain
Of this untested very risky ordeal,
But as the plane flew low above the train
He dropped sweetly onto that fast moving steel,

Across the rocking rooves he was jumping
To the cab where he grabbed for the brakes,
The wrecked bridge was quickly approaching
Dan knew there was no room for mistakes.

With brakes applied wheels started to squeal
Dan was elated he knew he would make it,
He was hanging over the canyon that was the deal
That million was already stashed in his pocket.

He was number one and now everyone knew
He had only done it because of his pride,
He leapt out of the cab to the cheers of the crew
But sadly for Dan he leapt out the wrong side.

One side of the train was against the opposite track
But the other looked straight down the ravine,
Dan leapt out into space with no way back
And that was the last time he was ever seen.

They never found any of poor Dan's remains
Just his ring on which was this inscription,
'Everything's possible I maintain
If done with enough conviction.'

Against all odds he'd finished the show
And his elation went to his head,
The cheers from the crowd fed his ego
He made one small mistake and was dead.

They say you should look before you leap
In Dan's case it was literally true,
At least he hadn't sold his life too cheap
Because to the million he was still due.

Just take this lesson from this tragic story
Of the demise of Dangerous Dan Mcgan,
Don't ignore common sense for the glory
You could end up dead and forgotten like Dan.

THE TALE OF DANIEL DEES
Pride comes before a fall

This is the story of Daniel Dees
Who was addicted to climbing trees.
When only two his mum declares
Daniel was climbing legs of chairs,
At four when not in playpen stabled
He was climbing legs of tables,
At five he progressed to chests of drawers
And hanging from the top of doors.
As he grew older his arms grew long
And his hands grew big and strong,
But crowning glory of his physique
Was a pair of large prehensile feet,
Those feet enabled him with ease
To pursue his hobby of climbing trees.
He set about with rare desire
To climb all the trees in Lincolnshire.
He climbed the ash, oak and sycamore,
Each one taller than the one before,
Then on the edge of Windy Wood
An enormous giant redwood stood.
He thought maybe it was too high
It seemed to reach up to the sky,
But it was there he couldn't resist
This opportunity could not be missed.
So he started to climb up off the ground
With no thought of how he'd get back down.
Up and up into this great tree
Climbed the foolish Daniel Dee.
He passed the point where birds were nesting,
Which he found quite interesting,
But soon his head was in the clouds
Far above the assembled crowds,
Who'd gathered below in expectation
Of Daniels impending hospitalization.

Above the clouds Daniel kept climbing
Up to where the sun was shining,
He soon reached such a high domain
He waved to a passing aero plane.
He made the mistake of looking down
And found he couldn't see the ground,
So forgetting view so panoramic
Daniel Dees started to panic.
Then while staring at defeat
He remembered his prehensile feet
He found hanging upside-down from branches
Considerably enhanced his chances,
As by hanging upsidedownward
He was always looking upward,
So to bring an end to this event
Daniel started his descent.

By this time it was getting dark
And waiting crowds had left the park.
Meanwhile at the local zoo
A keeper had set out to pursue
A lady gorilla that in a fit of rage
Had made a bid for freedom from her cage.
Armed with tranquilizer darts
Keeper Peter headed to wooded parts
Where he hoped that he would see
His gorilla escapee.
Hearing rustling in the wood
He hastened there fast as he could
And looking up by lucky chance
Saw his quarry hanging from a branch.
That's a gorilla for sure said Pete
Because it's hanging by its feet,
Not knowing it was Daniel Dees
High up there in the redwood tree.
Pete took aim and shot his darts
Right into Daniel's softest parts
Putting Daniel straight to sleep
Preventing him his hold to keep.

He fell with fast acceleration
Towards inevitable annihilation,
But Daniel, the lucky bleeder
Fell on top of keeper Peter,
Who, screaming like a squashed Chinchilla,
Attracted the said escaped gorilla,
Who to the spot a path did beat
Where she spotted Daniel's prehensile feet.
Thinking it was another of her kind
And with procreation on her mind,
She picked up sleepy Daniel Dees
And headed back into the trees.
Some people said it was on this day
He became the gorilla's fiancé.

The keeper searched both high and low
Even in the sewage overflow,
Into every hiding place he peered
But gorilla and Dan had disappeared.
So no one had seen poor Daniel Dees
Since he disappeared into the trees,
Until one day Daniel reappeared
Oh how all the townsfolk cheered.
He made a living making speeches
About how hard a gorilla's life is
But all they wanted to know about his life
Was did they live as man and wife?
As there had been much speculation
About potential copulation.
Daniel about this was quite coy
He'd always been a quiet boy
All he'd say about Priscilla,
Which is what he called his tame gorilla,
Was that if you ever happen to meet
A child with hairy hands and prehensile feet
Just remember to be kind
You never know it may be mine!

Don't bite off more than you can chew

Tom wanted to be an animal trainer
He owned a poodle black and cute,
Which he'd trained to walk on its hind legs
And perform a Nazi salute.

He thought he had a rapport with animals
And some of his friends may have agreed,
When they observed his poor table manners
And the casual way that he peed.

So when the circus came into the town
Tom was the first one into the tent
Where he tried to persuade the ring master
Of his animal training intent.

As it happened the circus was short of a trainer
For the contortionist cockatiels,
But ringmaster decided to give Tom a trial
As the trainer looking after the seals.

By the time they reached their next venue
Tom said he thought his seals were ready to go,
Ringmaster said you'd better be good
Because the seals will open the show.

Come first day of the show the tent was packed
VIP's seated to reflect their success,
The mayor was there, his wife's ample bosoms
Making a break for freedom out of her dress.

The seals came out to perform their act
They were balancing balls on their noses,
Standing up on their tails on tangerine tubs
In all sorts of provocative poses.

Tom then sought to involve the audience
Throwing balls to those in front row seats,
The seals then set off to retrieve them
And were rewarded with nice fishy treats.

All went well until he threw a ball to the mayor
One seal set off to where Mayor sat in the stalls,
But then it headed straight for his wife
Mistaking those large exposed bosoms for balls.

In a flash seal had dived into mayoress's cleavage
Until even its tail disappeared under her clothes
Then its head emerged from between her knees
With her bra balanced on the end of its nose.

Tom rushed over with a fish in his hand
To tempt the seal out from her silk foundation,
Seal wriggled out dragging her knickers down
So adding to her mortification.

The audience all thought it was part of the act
But their applause soon faded away,
When they saw the Mayoress was in some distress
Because her undies were now all on display.

Tom rescued the bra from the seal
And tried to return it to its proper place,
But mayor thought Tom was molesting his wife
And head-butted poor Tom in the face.

This ended Tom's career as a seal handler
But then he was given the horses to train,
But he'd find horses wouldn't do his bidding
Because they had no respect for his brain.

When Tom got the horses into the ring
They at first trotted around good as gold,
Until he cracked his big whip at their leader
When his next disaster began to unfold.

As one the horses turned to the audience
Rearing up as if begging for treats,
Then they let go a stream of steaming urine
And washed five small boys right out of their seats.

Regaining control Tom jumped astride the mare
Who decided she would join the protest,
Turning her back to the audience and lifting her tail
She crapped in the lap of a VIP guest.

Ringmaster was now at the end of his tether
He had to get rid of Tom tout de suite,
Tom had to be stopped before his destruction
Of their reputation was really complete.

Then next day he had a brilliant idea
He'd make Tom his next lion tamer,
So he put it to Tom who loved the idea
Ringmaster made Tom sign a disclaimer.

Ringmaster knew well a lion tamer's employment
Had proved very short lived in the past,
He wasn't sure how he'd explain that to Tom
But luckily Tom never asked.

The very next day Tom met his Lions
And found them a most friendly pride,
The big one promised not to behave badly
With his mouth open and Tom's head inside.

Tom was excited about his first performance,
And with his red uniform was really thrilled
Even when they explained colour was chosen
So it wouldn't show any blood that was spilled.

At first the show was going like clockwork
Tom was bathing in the audience's applause
Ringmaster admitted although Tom was an idiot
He certainly did have balls.

Then came the moment of truth for Tom
His head went into lion's mouth and from inside
Tom said, remember you promised not to hurt me,
I know said the lion …………..but I lied!

With that lion bit poor Tom's head clean off
Which goes to show if you set out to train,
It's no good just having the balls for the job
If you can't back that up with a brain.

THE STORY OF BRIAN BANE
Ignorance is bliss

This is the story of Brian Bane
The man with only half a brain.
One day when he was short of cash
Resulting from stock market crash
He heard this advert on the radio,
'If you want to see your money grow
Why not sell to us your body parts
We need livers, kidneys, lungs and hearts.'
Being of limited intellect
Brian thought if that's correct
It could be the answer to my plight.
So when he went back home that night
He sat straight down to make a list
Of his body parts that wouldn't be missed.
He started with his feet and toes
But thought when standing I need those
Need legs for walking and what's more,
Without them bum's too close to the floor.
Hands and arms likewise required
When on his cycle rubber tyred,
Wanting to signal, as he might
That he was turning left or right.
As Brian was very keen on food
When liver and stomach he reviewed,
He eliminated them from parts selection
As they were essential for his digestion.
If bladder, kidneys and bowel I loose
There'd be problems with number ones and twos.
Private parts may well be needed
In unlikely event that I succeeded
With my girlfriend Brenda Brace
In finally getting past second base.
As for my appendix and my spleen,
In there somewhere but never seen,
I must admit I am not sure
What these bits are really for.

As for my lungs and heart
These are I think essential parts
Without which even he had read
He'd be well and truly dead.
Then Brian thought is it insane
To think of selling half my brain?
He was sure he didn't need it all
Because as far as he recalled
Teachers at school were always saying,
When exam results surveying,
That as far as we can tell
A boy with half a brain would do as well.
So that's it thought Brian, brain it is
Right or wrong decision was his,
It wasn't operation that he dreaded
Just wondered if he'd feel a bit light headed.

So next day Brian went to meet,
In consulting rooms in Regent Street,
The doctor offering him this service
Who said to Brian don't be nervous.
First of all we'll do a scan
And we'll be as careful as we can
To only take that part of brain
Which we think you won't need again.
Brian lay down on a comfy bed
While the doctors scanned his head,
Doctor looked somewhat bemused
Saying this brain looks hardly used
Consultant agreed saying I've seen a few
But this brain really looks brand new,
I haven't seen one in this condition
Since I operated on that politician.
Surgeon said once we start we can't stop
I've decided to take it from the top,
Brian said wait, not so fast
And for his cash up front he asked.
Pocketing the sizeable wad
They put Brian into land of nod.

Then lying him down upon the bed
They sawed off top of Brian's head,
Took out some brain and with instant glue
Stuck skull back on as good as new.
Brian woke up pocket full of cash
Thinking he'd been a little rash,
Because although not feeling any pain
In a nearby jar floated half his brain.
Of what he actually had done
Memory of this he just had none,
Doctor said, 'fraid that's how it'll be
You sold to us your memory.
Brian realizing he was in a mess
Had to look in his wallet for his address.

Because of the past he had no sense
He only lived in the present tense.
Didn't know if he was Christian or atheist
A fighter or a pacifist,
And very much to his relief
He had no political belief,
At future dinner party occasions
He'd be spared dull conversations.
Of his personal history, he had no clue
So every experience he had was new.
He never felt guilty about what he'd done
So found he had a lot more fun.
One problem arising from Brian's state
Was he found that he was gaining weight
Because he'd make a meal eat it and then
He'd cook and eat same meal again.
Brian realised where no memory exists
His life would be run by writing lists.
Another problem of his condition
Conversations were mainly repetition,
Poor Brian would never again
Enjoy a song with a refrain.
He never remembered loans he made
So never asked for them to be repaid.

Brian was the most unusual friend
He would never borrow but always lend.
All of his relatives he disregards
Saving a fortune on birthday cards.
With his own birthday he couldn't engage
Because he didn't know his age.
He never yearned for the past or reminisced
For him nostalgia didn't exist.
So Brian lived his life free of care
Because he was totally unaware
Of anything he'd done or said
Or anything he'd seen or read,
Whether he'd come home a little tight
Or who he'd slept with the previous night.
Brian was neither happy nor sad
About the operation that he'd had.
He didn't worry, not one bit
Because he couldn't remember it.
Poor Brian with memory departed
Couldn't even remember how it started,
So apart from running his life with lists
Brian Bane's brain was hardly missed

WATER

A drop of water is worth more than gold to a thirsty man

Water is a common compound in our universe
The life forms it supports are many and diverse,
Too little and the earth's a desert desolate and brown,
Too much and earth floods causing some to drown.

One week without water and the human body dies
So water is important to our daily lives,
We need two liters every day to keep our body well
And as much again to wash in if we aren't to smell.

Water forms the oceans across both hemispheres
From the Antarctic wastes to the shores around Tangiers.
We love to eat the fish that in the ocean swim
But are scared of sharks that can amputate a limb.

Water that forms the rivers flowing out into the sea
It is always changing but looks the same to you or me.
Bridges cross those rivers that are very deep and wide
Providing both a spectacle and an aid to suicide.

Water forms waterfalls and bubbling cascades
From which we see mist rising and rainbows that are made,
They're used as a backdrop for romantic pictures
And are now one of our favourite garden features.

Water forms the rain that falls in the summer showers
Drops resting like diamonds on the petals of the flowers,
Providing something special to the English nation
A never ending topic of noncommittal conversation.

Water forms the snowflakes ethereal and mystical
Their designs are infinite, each one an individual.
Snow provides the ski slopes that give us a winter thrill
But also forms the avalanche that can destroy and kill.

Water plumps the grapes used to make wine and sherry
And delicious strawberries, raspberries and cherries.
It also makes those sugary drinks with zero alcoholicity
Which give us diabetes and contribute to obesity.

Water forms the tears flowing from the misty eyes
Of lovers at the station, saying their goodbyes,
Tears lubricate our eyes and do many other things
But can be a real nuisance when cutting onion rings.

Water is in the clouds above and in the earth below
It's clever stuff, this compound we know as H_2O.
Heat takes it up into the clouds through evaporation
And when it falls down again it's called precipitation.

Water is the only compound within earth's ambient range
That can exist as solid, liquid or a gas with atoms rearranged.
Expanding into steam inside engines thermodynamic
It powered the Flying Scotsman and sadly the Titanic.

So give thanks to those covalent bonds holding H and O together
Without them we'd go thirsty and wouldn't get any weather,
We'd have nothing left to talk about and not so much to eat
You must admit as a compound water is difficult to beat.

THE DENTIST
The limit of every pain is an even greater pain

With a ping it arrives on your phone
That most unwelcome text,
It's not only the message that worries you
But what you know is coming next.

Could you please ring for an appointment
Your dental check-up is now due?
You think about ignoring it
But you know just what they'll do.

You will eventually get a phone call
And they won't accept excuses,
They don't let anyone escape
Whatever reason patient uses.

So you fix a date and it is done
All too soon the day is here,
Your feet drag you to the dentist
Your smile holding back your fear.

You sit in the waiting room
Trying to hide your nervous state,
Playing with your mobile phone
Glad they are running late.

Then the invitation comes
Nurse says please follow me
Into that room with just one chair
You're never pleased to see.

There follows usual examination
Recording state of teeth and gum
In a secret language which prevents you
Knowing of procedures yet to come.

Maxillary laterals and cuspids
Mandibular central too
Cavity in twenty upper left,
There seemed an awful lot to do.

The dentist's jacket has short sleeves
And you note with satisfaction
The large size of his biceps
Needed for rapid tooth extraction.

He asked about my allergies
In the event I should complain,
I replied only thing I'm allergic to
Is unnecessary pain.

You lie there prone upon the couch
Mouth open in anticipation
While dentist with pick and mirror
Assesses decay situation.

From the dentist's cruel lips
Escapes a sigh of satisfaction
As he spots one of my teeth
With signs of putrefaction.

This won't need anesthetic
Said dentist with a smirk,
I could tell by how he held the drill
He was happy in his work.

You may feel a slight discomfort
The kindly dentist said,
But we all know that he really means
Pain will leave you nearly dead.

The drill sets up its fiendish whine
My buttocks clench in anticipation
Then the smell of burning tooth
Signals start of operation.

Just put your hand up dentist said
If it starts to hurt
But I couldn't feel any pain
So relaxed my hold upon his shirt.

But then he hit the nerve
He held me down with his legs astride,
I would have bitten his fingers off
But he'd wedged mouth open wide.

I tried to give vent to a scream
But he had five fingers in my gob
And the only sound that I could make
Was a strangulated sob.

Then he put his drill down
I sat up as he released his grip,
I haven't finished yet he said
And escapes not in the script.

But the worst was over
Just the filling still to feel
Except I couldn't talk or swallow
With a mouth still full of steel.

Do you think dentists are all sadists
Who take a special pride
Trying to make you answer questions
With your mouth wedged open wide?

A little of compound number two
He asked nurse for a start,
Then got to work molding it
Into a piece of dental art.

Just give your mouth a swill
Said dentist with a smile,
I think your teeth should now
Be alright for a while.

I smiled wanly at him
Because what is there to say,
To one who inflicts an hour of pain
For which he makes you pay.

I don't know if it's down to God
Or due to evolution,
But having teeth that rot and ache
Is an unsatisfactory solution.

I can't claim to be an expert
But cannot help but feel,
It would have been a better job
If teeth were made of stainless steel.

Memory has faded now
Maybe it wasn't all that bad,
But I still have the feeling
It wasn't the best day that I've had.

This is the story of Sally Sweet
Who wasn't happy with her feet,
She was happy with her knees and thighs
But thought her feet too large a size.

She didn't think one so petite
Should be standing on two size ten feet.
As she wouldn't get much taller
She'd have to make her two feet smaller.

She went to see a doctor Twist
A very famous podiatrist,
Said doc what can you do with those
I'd like heels closer to my toes?

Doc said I'll see what I can do
By finding some new feet for you,
When new size has been calculated
Your old feet will be amputated.

When feet are precisely matched
New smaller feet will be attached,
Sounds very good said Sally Sweet,
I'm fed up with these ugly feet.

Some weeks passed then doctor Twist,
Having searched all spare feet that exist,
Said my search is now complete
I've found a pair of size three feet.

As soon as Sally got the news
She bought ten pairs of size three shoes,
And dreamed of walking down her street
Balancing on her size three feet.

Next day she turned up for operation
And underwent the amputation,
Then unconscious Sally Sweet
Was fitted with her size three feet.

Awaking from the Anesthetic
She started waxing quite poetic,
I just can't wait till I expose
My new ten tiny little toes.

I'll go tippy tapping down the street
On my new dainty little feet,
I can't wait to see how it feels
To wear some nice stiletto heels.

A few weeks later, she was seen
In her size three shoes sparkly clean,
Entering the local supermarket
Looking to fill her shopping basket.

Then music came over the loudspeakers
Causing strange stirrings in Sally's sneakers,
As down the aisle she sought to advance
Her new feet broke into a dance.

Dancing a tango, she couldn't stop
She tangoed her way right out the shop.
Without the music her dancing halted
Leaving poor Sally quite exhausted.

Sally soon found that her new feet
Danced when she heard a rhythmic beat,
She danced wherever she might be
Even when in the lavatory.

Sometimes a quickstep sometimes samba,
A waltz, a foxtrot or a rumba,
An arabesque or a pirouette
Bringing our Sally out in a sweat.

Sally thought something's amiss
With these new feet from doctor Twist,
So off she went for a consultation
To tell Twist of her situation.

She said, doc something isn't right
My feet are dancing day and night,
Please doc can you be my saviour
And modify my feet's behavior?

Then doc provided her the answer
He'd given her feet of a ballroom dancer,
Solution is, doctor explained
Your new feet must be retrained.

Saying there was no time to lose
He provided her with special shoes,
These will stop you dancing, doctor said
Because these shoes are made of lead.

Doc was right when music sounded
Sally's feet stayed firmly grounded,
Although if music reached concert pitch
She found her knees would start to twitch.

But walking caused quite a kerfuffle
Poor Sally Sweet could only shuffle,
She couldn't run now anymore
Without leaving big holes in the floor.

When boarding aircraft they made her wait
Then loaded her with all the freight,
And she created quite a fuss
When getting on the local bus.

Sitting on back seat, Sally found
She lifted front wheels off the ground.
Conductor said, to solve this riddle
I'll have to sit you in the middle.

I cannot understand at all
How someone so heavy can be so small,
Until this mystery you unravel
Afraid you must restrict your travel.

Sally wore the shoes for six months straight
And carrying all that extra weight,
Which she was desperate to escape,
Had given Sally an hourglass shape.

Although this provided untold joy
To every nearby teenage boy
Romantic relationships didn't advance
Because the poor girl couldn't dance.

At last her podiatric proff.
Said it's time to take shoes off,
She grabbed left shoe and off it came
Then with the right shoe did the same.

Her feet now felt as light as air
Almost as if they were not there,
Without lead shoes everyone agreed
Sally's feet moved at tremendous speed.

Now she was feeling so energetic
She joined the local club athletic
And very soon to her surprise
Won the hundred metres prize.

She was so good soon she was seen
By head of the Olympics team,
This well-known running connoisseur
Said this girls feet are just a blur.

To the Olympics we must take her
I'm sure she is a record breaker,
She joined the team and won the gold
Her story has often been retold.

The tale of how little Sally Sweet
The girl who had replacement feet,
Had overcame her foot fixation
To become the darling of the nation.

She was now seen on the TV screens
Advertising tight designer jeans,
Fitness clubs and margarines
And fast automobile machines.

Then we all know how it goes
She was a guest on TV panel shows,
She wanted to make some money fast
Not knowing how long fame would last.

Sally ended up with a handsome spouse
Living in a stylish country house,
But she never forgot, did Sally Sweet,
She owed it all to her replacement feet.

ERNIE THE EARTHWORM

The early bird gets the worm, the early worm gets eaten

I'm an earthworm called Ernie
But no one ever hears me
Because I live deep underground
And I never make any sound.
It's not an easy life you know
Crawling through earth everywhere I go.

I don't have any legs or feet
So I'll never be an athlete,
I don't have any arms or hands
So I won't be joining any bands,
I can't speak and I can't see
Life's not much fun for a worm like me.

I spend my life hiding in small holes
Because I'm a favorite food of moles,
When rain falls down from the sky
I come to the surface, don't know why,
That is a dangerous place I feel
When you're a blackbird's favorite meal.

I'm a hermaphrodite but for my health
I must not make love to myself,
I must lie head to tail with another
Who for all I know could be my brother.
My life is one that's full of toil
Turning vegetation into soil.

In three weeks with great fecundity
I produce three hundred progeny,
Which is a very good thing, isn't it
When a bird can eat you in one minute?
And one ton of earthworms can consume
One ton of rubbish really soon.

Whilst slugs and snails, unlike me,
Are both the gardener's enemy
I have become the gardener's friend
By making soil come out my end.
I don't even have to chew it
In fact I don't know how I do it.

That's typical of the poor worm's plight
To be liked just only for their shite!
But at wriggling, I am a master
I don't know anything that wriggles faster,
But despite my talent I'm upset
I've not been on talent show yet.

Even though I've got two brains
I can't ride bikes and can't drive trains,
But I've been to school and then to college
When my two brains absorbed the knowledge.
What use is that I hear you say?
Well I'll write a book on worms one day.

I'll record all the wormy things I do,
I'll call the book 'A Worm's Eye View,'
Or maybe when it's written down
I'll call it 'Fifty Shades of Brown.'
I don't think of God or the creation
Or prayer or Buddhist meditation.

How can you believe in evolution
A worm can't be the final solution?
How can evolution have got it right
Producing an armless, legless hermaphrodite?
But there is something you should know
If I'm cut in half, I don't regrow,
No I die, that's just how worms are made
So watch what you're doing with that ruddy spade.

THE STORY OF LARRY LANES
Better safe than sorry

This is the story of Larry Lanes
Who had a fear of aero planes,
Whenever his job meant he must fly
He always thought that he would die.
He said if man was meant to be in the air
He'd be given wings by Him up there.
In Darwin's theory of evolution
Wings were not seen as our solution,
No it gave us feet to get around
While staying firmly on the ground.
When Larry was forced by work to travel
To lands across the English Channel
He approached the plane with trepidation
As from his engineering occupation
He was very much aware
That aircraft were heavier than air.
They could not float like a balloon
But this metal tube would very soon
Through unknown forces they called lift,
Generated from speed so very swift,
Be sucked high up into the air
And by some magic held up there.
Larry thought it even more cruel
To surround him with explosive fuel.
Strapped in his seat with hundreds more
Confined there by an air locked door
What's the first thing that they do?
One member of the aircraft's crew
Stands up completely unabashed
Telling you what to do in event we crash.
Put your head between your legs
To protect your face and toothy pegs,
Not much help Larry decides
'Cause he knows jet planes don't glide.

So he spends his time when in the air
Wishing that he wasn't there
Listening for every different sound
Which might mean plane was going down,
Dreading turbulence which among other things
Can break off tails and tear off wings.
Despite fast beating heart and sweaty palm
He sits there looking very calm
Because he's one of the frequent flyer set
Who've seen it all and aren't upset,
Whether the weather's rough or fine
He casually sits there sipping wine.
Even when one day captain reports
One engine is rather out of sorts
Which in fact he soon discovered
That said engine was totally buggered.
Despite turmoil going on inside
Larry reassured passenger at his side
That it was designer's contention
Plane could fly on just one engine.
I don't care said fellow flyer
About the claims of the designer,
We're only halfway to our destination
And have lost half of our motivation.
In these engine circumstances
I don't give that much for our chances
Of crossing this ocean, because I think
We are going to end up in the drink.
Don't worry said Larry I always expect it
That's why we're sat by emergency exit.
Despite Larry's apparent carefree stance
He had to go to toilet and change his pants.
Larry was relieved again in another way
When plane landed safely in LA.
He resolved right there never again
Would he travel in an aero plane,
And booked the ticket for his return trip
Larry was going home by ship.

THE BILL
Every man has his price

This is the story of dining out
With the upwardly mobile set,
Not so much about the food and drink
As hostilities with wine and baguette.

We received an invitation to dinner
From some people down the street,
They'd arranged the date with friends
And picked a place where we could eat.

The wife asked what she should wear
Was it casual or was it smart,
Or was it just smart casual saying,
I have to know before we start.

She asked me to check the menu
By looking it up on the internet
The price of the starters would tell me
The sort of clientele they'd get.

I had a quick look at the prices
It was as plain as the nose on your face
That only the smartest designer clothes
Would do in that sort of place.

After squeezing the wife into her Spanx
And ten changes of dress, if not more,
I brushed down my suit and was ready
The taxi waiting there at the door.

They were all there at the table
The Wills, the Knotts and the Wrights,
And not forgetting the Robertson Smythes
Who were the high class guests of the night.

After ten minutes forthright discussion
It was decided we'd all eat a la carte,
But the menu was all written in French
That hacked us off for a start.

It took time for us to work out
What was a Plat de Jour or Entrée,
And the difference between
The Plat Principal and the Specialité.

Then we were given a large red book
Turned out it was just the wine list,
In the time taken to decide what to drink
We'd normally already be pissed.

All this decision making had left us
Hungry and with a raging thirst,
But I couldn't help but wonder
If food or death would find us first.

When the starters finally arrived
The portions were rather meager
We tried to fill ourselves up on the bread
Without appearing over eager.

Served rather more for appearance than taste
Food wasn't really worth the expense,
But everyone said it was delicious
So we joined in the pretence.

All in all not too bad an evening
Not bad that is until,
When the meal was over
Came the time to settle the bill.

Easy way was to add in the tip
And divide the bill by ten
But oh no that was much too simple
So we started debating again.

The Wills said they would not agree
It was all wrong said the Wrights,
The Knotts said they just could not,
Nothing satisfied the Robertson Smythes.

Mrs. Wills said she only had soup as a starter,
Knots said difference in price of paté was small,
The Robertson Smythes had smoked salmon,
Mr. Wright hadn't had a starter at all.

The Robertson Smythes pointed out the Wrights
Had had fillet steak for their mains
While they'd only had fish and a salad
Which balanced out their supposed gains.

Most of us had cheese and coffee
The Robertson Smythes had a liqueur,
For which Mrs. Wills said she wouldn't pay
If it was left up to her.

The Knotts were Methodist teetotalers
So did not partake of the wine
And weren't prepared to contribute
To all the others moral decline.

Mr. Knott was the local headmaster
True to form of the bill took control
He had a degree in mathematics
So was a natural to take on this role.

Out came his handheld computer
A spreadsheet was soon on display,
And in only forty-five minutes
He'd calculated what each diner should pay.

Mr. Knott said he'd rounded up to nearest pound
Mr. Wright said that's wrong, it would be best
If all of the figures were rounded down
And Robertson Smythes paid for the rest.

After all of our deliberations
About who'd eaten what at what cost,
The spreadsheet showed if we'd all paid a tenth
Then no one would really have lost.

We'd found the whole process exhausting
And decided right there and then,
To never again go to dinner
Where bill had to be divided by ten.

We'd stick to a meal down the local pub
Where the only decisions you had to make
Was whether the wine was red or a white,
And was it fish and chips or a steak.

THE PARTY
A party without cake is just a meeting

It's that time of year again
When you mix lager and Bacardi,
When you over eat and over drink
It's the office Christmas party.

How can it be that time again?
How can it come round so soon?
I swear it seems like yesterday
That it was only June.

I'm not a great one for parties
I'm unsociable I guess
At least at Christmas I am spared
From having to go in fancy dress.

First you must visit the card shop
All stars and snowy churches
And inside all those sentimental
Cloying mawkish verses.

One for the managers and senior staff
Secretaries and tea lady too,
And all the others who surely will
Send a Christmas card to you.

And what a price these bits of card
It's becoming quite absurd
Did Picasso paint the picture?
Did McCartney write the words?

Once you have parted with the money,
And the bill is far from small,
The job is still not finished
Until you've written in them all.

What is the message you can write
Apart from saying you're still alive,
And of all the pills you're taking
In order to survive.

No holidays to brag about
No genius grandchild to pretend
Just the passing of another year
And the death of another friend.

The office Christmas party's held
To heal departmental divides,
But usually ends in open warfare
Between the opposing sides.

I try to think of some excuses
Claiming ill health is tempting fate,
Or maybe because of advancing years
I could simply forget the date.

But I know there's no escape
From this annual occasion
So we set off in the evening
To the Christmas party destination.

There everyone is gathered
Full of cheer and Bon Homie,
All full of Christmas spirit
And the miserable one .... that's me.

The design of all their sweaters
Leaves much to be desired
Leaving me thinking if I'd been right
That fancy dress was not required.

I was still quite unpopular
Much to my satisfaction,
As I moved inside the younger staff
All took avoiding action.

I trapped a few against the bar
Enjoying their apprehension,
Trying not to say any words
Which would relieve the tension.

I picked on one of the salesmen
Saying with company sales declining,
Did he not think he should be selling
Not against this hotel bar reclining?

The others laughed with some relief
Not at my witty repartee,
What they thought inside their head
Was I'm glad he didn't pick on me.

So I passed a pleasant hour
Reading staff names on lapel labels,
Preventing their enjoyment
Just as far as I was able.

Everyone sat down at the table
In order of seniority,
I couldn't help but notice it was
The inverse of capability.

They tried to make me wear a hat
And were annoyed when I declined,
Declaring that hats were something
For which my head was not designed.

We all set about the food with gusto
The waiters all huffed and puffed,
And after only half an hour it wasn't just
The turkey that was stuffed.

So there we sat feeling slightly sick
We'd all been rather greedy,
Giving no thought to the starving
Or to the poor and needy.

We had all succeeded through
Our intemperate Christmas function,
In maximising our carbon footprint
Through conspicuous consumption.

We'd destroyed all the crackers
Groaned at all the jokes,
Comforted by the feeling
We were just like all the other folks.

I noticed things were getting rowdy
Due to quantity of drink consumed,
Staff were gathering in corners
Where my old failures would be exhumed.

It looked to me the time had come
For me to quietly slip away
I don't think that many noticed
Or at least they didn't say.

That's it for another year
No more parties to attend,
I can go back to being a boss again
And stop pretending to be friends.

But all too soon with advancing years
The season of turkey and tangerines,
Will present all the old dilemmas
Unless .... death intervenes.

EXCESSIVE WIND
A Vegan's Lament

To eat or not to eat that was the question
For the man with inadequate digestion,
Cauliflower, sprouts, beans and cabbage
Were the foods that did the damage.
Whether raw or cooked or tinned,
They generated excessive wind.
This is what caused embarrassment
To poor old Ronald Ruminant

For Ronald problem was not good
Because he really loved his food
Ever since he was in his teens
Ronald really loved his greens.
Greens were almost all he ate
Regardless of what was on his plate
Chicken, pork, lamb and beef
Were too much trouble for his teeth.

When he was a child his mother said
Eat your greens or you'll wind up dead.
Ronald didn't need such exhortation
To consume his allotted vegetation,
After downing his portion at faster rate
He cleared up brother and sister's plate,
And far from finding this distasteful
His two siblings were always grateful.

Mother too was very satisfied
That greens were good for Ron's inside,
Until she detected an unpleasant whiff
That caused her nose to twitch and sniff.
Everyone was searching for cause of smell
But where it came from they couldn't tell
Until one day it became quite·clear

Smell was stronger when Ron was near.
To try and make smell go away
They made poor Ron bathe every day,
They tried every deodorant that existed
But the pong from Ron still persisted.
His brother found the explanation
Through his nighttime observation,
I have the answer, brother grinned
Ron is continually breaking wind.

The odour was from Ron alas
He was generating too much gas,
Ron's mum made correct assumption
It was due to excessive greens consumption.
They told him his diet was just for rabbits
But Ron wouldn't change his eating habits,
As last resort in desperation
They made Ron live in isolation.

On his own Ron sought to find
Something to occupy his mind
He wondered if he could find a way
To make his farting prowess pay.
Maybe he could make a quid
By feeding farts into the national grid,
Or maybe he could spend his afternoons
Blowing up hot air balloons.

Then he saw one of YouTube shows
A man playing a trombone with his nose
He not only played a haunting blues
But generated over a million views.
Ron thought that gent he could surpass
Playing trumpet using his excess gas,
So with a trumpet lodged in anal cavity
He played the trumpet voluntary.

He became another YouTube sensation
With his gas and trumpet combination,
He expanded his music repertoire
By accompanying himself on his guitar.
He had some trousers specially made
So his bottom parts were not displayed,
His fame was such he was asked to go
Onto the Royal Variety show.

Performing for the upper classes
Ron didn't want to run out of gasses
So on the night to remove all doubts
Ron ate two extra plates of sprouts.
So fully fueled he wowed the crowd
He was tooting his trumpet very loud,
Then halfway through a movement by Purcell
Ron felt his stomach start to swell.

Buildup of gas inside his tum
Could only be relieved via Ron's bum,
As the gas started to escape
At an ever and ever faster rate
Trumpet note became very shrill
Notes went higher then higher still,
Until those royals, peers and sirs
Had to hold their fingers in their ears.

Then as the sound started breaking glass
Pressure exceeded grip of poor Ron's ass,
The trumpet shot out of Ronald's bum
Right out across the auditorium.
Straight as an arrow, trumpet fled
Knocking sparkly tiara off Queens head,
Ron was in shock until someone said
It's OK Ron, the Queen's not dead.

Ron gave up show business right away
And changed his diet that very day,
He'd given his backside too much exposure
Ron's farting days were over.
And although he's back at home again
Ron still thinks back to those days when
He was famous, it made him ponder
If absence makes the fart grow fonder.

So if you receive an invitation
To Ron's house, don't go with trepidation,
Because now there is very little chance
You'll experience any flatulence,
Because our Ronald has been reformed
His eating habits totally transformed,
It's been for Ronald a brand new start
He's had *a total eclipse of the fart.*

THE ITCH

Pain is easier to endure than an itch

This is the story of Philomena Fitch
Who developed a very annoying itch
In a place where she could not get at it
Which meant that she couldn't scratch it.
In order to reach this annoying spot
She required supple limbs she had not got
She twisted her body this way and that,
Watched all the while by her Tabby cat
Who seemed able with annoying ease,
When searching for invading fleas,
To reach every part of its anatomy
In a way which defied reality.
Twisting half his body left the other right
He could see bits normally out of sight,
And with an elegantly executed twitch
Could stretch out its leg and scratch the itch.

But poor Philomena wasn't blessed
With flexibility that cat possessed,
She looked around for any aids
To reach the itch between her shoulder blades.
She looked inside the kitchen drawer
Didn't know what half the things were for,
Tried everything but no matter which
They were all too short to reach the itch.
This itch was getting really bad
And was driving poor Philomena mad,
Off to the doctor went Philomena
And as soon as doctor seen her
He said that's as bad an itch as I have seen
And gave her a great big jar of cream,
Use this cream the doctor said
Each night before you go to bed.

That night Philomena stood, without a stitch
Determined to sort out her itch
But of course silly girl soon found
Whichever way she turned around
She had same problem as before
Spot was itching even more.
She let out a frustrated scream
She couldn't reach the spot to spread the cream,
But she would not be defeated
Itchy spot had to be treated.

Muttering a secret prayer
She went out onto top of stair
And on the posts protruding knob
Philomena put a blob
Of the cream doctor provided,
Then turned around till it coincided
With that dratted itchy spot,
But however she tried she could not
Get the needed distribution
Then decided on solution.
She would apply much bigger blob
To the stairs protruding knob.

As she did some fell upon the stair
But she didn't see it there
And as she turned herself around
She slipped on cream upon the ground.
And with a scream Philomena Fitch
Wearing nothing, not a stitch
Slid down the stairs upon her back
Each step giving her a whack.
At the bottom when she arose
And started putting on her clothes
Although her back was very sore
Her spot wasn't itching any more.

It seemed like she had found a cure
In a step by step way that's for sure.
Just by chance a few days later
At her local cut price trader
Right there hanging from a rack
Was a scratcher for your back.
Just what Philomena needed
For her itch which had preceded,
She took it home with beating heart
Waiting for the itch to start.

Being Yorkshire girl by birth
She wanted to get her money's worth,
So she sat in anticipation
Of returning irritation.
But as the hours turned into days
And her itch still stayed away
Philomena stored back scratcher
As for now it didn't seem to matter.
If that damned itch did return
She wouldn't be the least concerned
She'd be able to scratch it from the start
Her scratcher could reach every part.

So it is poor Philomena Fitch
Is sitting there without her itch
Bemoaning the fact she had to pay
To scratch an itch that got away.

THOUGHTS FROM A SMALL TOWN BAR
Of course I drink, I'm a writer!

Sitting in a bar the other day
I was asked what I had to say
About the state of the railway station,
And if I believed in the Creation.
I said problem with station is trains are late,
Can you believe in Creation and in fate?
Anyhow it's no good asking me
I'm just about as dumb as you can be,
Ask a professor who knows everything
Who's forgotten more than I'm remembering.
I am sure that he will be able
To furnish you with graphs and tables,
To explain any problem big or small
Without using any facts at all.
As for me, my education
Provided very little information
Useful for answering any questions
About origins of life or railway stations.

I just came in for a beer to drink
To give myself some time to think
About the many unanswered questions,
Like who suggests auto suggestions?
Who was responsible for inventing sin?
And for the state the human race is in?
Without a god who will you pray to?
When you're lost who's going to save you?
Why are some too rich and some too poor?
What really goes on behind closed doors?
Why do tears flow when we cry?
What is it that holds up the sky?
Who was Captain Hook before he lost his hand?
And many other things I don't understand.

The world's full of questions without answers
Singers without songs music without dancers,
People with no talent in all the high places,
People wielding power with unknown faces.

People exploited just to make things cheap
Which others buy and never keep.
Obscene amounts paid to celebrities
Who lecture us on life's inequalities.
A tax exile telephoned from Lichtenstein
Said he'd do nothing for me if he only had the time.

We are all searching for an identity
Scared of ending life as a nonentity,
Looking for that fifteen minutes of fame
When some camera records our face and name,
For those fleeting moments we can feel
Our lives mean something, that we are real.
Because we travel by air, land and sea
We think this means that we are free,
But with the technological revolution
Our so called freedom is mere illusion.
Everything we do everywhere we go
Someone records it someone will know,
For the very first time in history
Our records will be kept for eternity,
Now through the magic of an internet portal
Like those Greek gods we are immortal.

Happiness though is not so easily found
What is missing is more profound,
Living life without envy without greed,
Only ever taking what you need,
Respect for the truth taking a stand,
Finding the love for your fellow man.
I leave the bar no wiser than when I came
Secure in only my thought and name,
I have absorbed no knowledge I can recall
Except that I know nothing at all.
I will live out my life in relative ignorance
In the arms of capricious circumstance,
Until it's time for me to finally go
To glory on high or the fires below.
One last thing on one last line,

The beer I had tasted just fine.

MISCELLANEOUS MUSINGS

*'Poetry heals the wounds
inflicted by reason.'*

Novalis

STATEMENT
The only meaning that is absolute is mine

I offer no excuses for any of my actions
It matters not if I am wrong or right,
Every word is written for my own satisfaction
I am in control of everything I write.

My poetry is not written to inspire you
My words not meant to lessen your distress,
I do not write to tell you that I love you,
I do not write to applaud you or protest.

I will not apologise for literary failures
I do not seek your approval or your praise,
I alone will answer for my behaviour
There is no dogma my actions have betrayed.

All the words I write have been discreetly hidden
Held safely in my mind ever since my youth,
No matter if they were sacred or forbidden
Only when written down had they any truth.

Don't ask their meaning they're just words I caught
As they fell like leaves in some ancient wood,
Fall in love with my thoughts and with their sound,
My words are better felt than understood.

If you see semantic errors don't waste breath
In querying my literary education,
I am more interested in love, life and death,
I am not so interested in the punctuation.

My poetry is written for myself and not for you
So my reasons for each word remain concealed,
Sometimes it goes beyond that which I can really do
Surprising me with the truths that are revealed.

I never wanted my verses to be holy psalms
They are not meant to be dissected or explored,
Their meaning isn't hidden but explicit
Not disguised within a dozen metaphors.

If you read my words and find that they offend you,
If you disagree with their sound and their intent,
If you feel deceived and disappointed,
You misinterpret the message that I've sent.

Should by chance my words serve to remind you
Of a past love you have come to redefine,
It is a random crossing of our experience
The only meaning that is absolute is mine.

I am a compilation of many contradictions
A pessimist holding hands with hope,
Resisting attacks from opponents of tradition
I was in control of everything I wrote.

GLASS DREAMS
She told me only love was truth

My dreams are brittle, they are glass
Don't hold onto them too tight,
You will break them and they'll shatter
Into the oblivion of the night.

She disclosed me then exposed me
Then guided me in-between
My deceit and my defiance
To the peace of the Nazarene.

She saw the sadness of my vanity
She told me only love was truth,
My pride vanished when she kissed me
Leaving a poem in my mouth.

She hid dark thoughts like contraband
In the secret caverns of her mind,
Loving me with a harlot's touch
Putting all my innocence behind.

I tasted her then she devoured me
She was my air, I breathed her in,
She redefined me and confined me
In the covert dungeon of her sin.

My passion sank without any trace
In the deep ocean of her love,
Her hand held out to catch the pieces
From my broken heart above.

I tried to discover her secret code
I tried to look behind her eyes,
But she clothed her dreams in camouflage
Even her words were in disguise.

Never disclosing any of her secrets
Like those Rosicrucians of the past,
She never gave me a single answer
Despite the hundred times I asked.

She said she knew my dreams were fragile
But that everything must pass,
And every dream we had ever dreamed
Would be shattered like the glass.

Leaving with no word of explanation
The affair just ended with a kiss,
A heart can find no healing consolation
Confronted with treachery like this.

That's how my dream of love was broken
Waking up alone with reality and pain,
I wished to breathe without the hurt
And never to fall in love again.

You can tell anyone who's looking for me
I'll be where the fallen angel screams,
In that place where martyred lovers lie
Amongst their shattered dreams.

INVITATION

Words like sour fruit in my mouth

I was invited to a festival
In a windswept hill top town
A festival of verse a poetry review.
They wanted me to read some lines
Which I had written down
In remembrance of someone I once knew.

The raw rough-hewn verses
Were recorded months before
On unread pages of a soon forgotten book,
Secured at the back of
Some rarely opened drawer
Hidden away from any casual look.

Some words you write are not
Meant for random disclosure
They are too personal, too arcane.
They were only of value
At the moment when I showed her,
They would not profit from being read again.

Too little time has passed
And I have not forgotten
Wounds unhealed still bleeding inside,
Too soon to walk that road
Where loved ones have fallen
Where heartache and heartbreak collide.

To stand alone in pain and silence
Surrounded by my fears
Words like sour fruit in my mouth.
The occasion would be no celebration
But a festival of tears,
An unwelcome confrontation with the truth.

I could not use those lines
For my or others satisfaction
That would be an act of selfish vanity,
There could be no other
Reason for such an action
But to convert my loss to a normality.

I told them I would have
To refuse the invitation
For then or any other tomorrow.
I would have to bury too much
Hurt for such a recitation,
And push aside too many memories of sorrow.

ONE NIGHT BAND.
You'll never know just how good crazy feels

The dance was over
The drunk and the sober
Were leaving to walk into the night,
The last of the sinners
The losers and winners
Exposing their dreams to reality's light.

Lonely love sick teens
Were leaving their dreams
On the floor with the litter and grime,
Where they would remain
Until picked up again
When the band came around the next time.

On the edge of the floor
With her back to the door
Stood a girl that real love had passed by,
She had turned down again
All the good looking men
She didn't trust them to not make her cry.

In her faded blue jeans
She was lost in her dreams
Heartache hidden behind a painted smile,
The eyes blue and clear
Held one unshed tear
But she carried her sadness with style.

She was searching for love
The sort the band had sung of
I took her arm, stepping into the street,
Told her she should not grieve
She must always believe
And she should never consider defeat.

I have to tell you, she said
Before you take me to bed
I've been cut deep by a lover's pretense,
Promises were made
But I was betrayed
My innocence insufficient defense.

She said I'm a train with no line
I am a clock without time
To me love's a stranger, love's an unknown,
She spoke of love's mystery
Her voice was like poetry
Some words were stolen, some words her own.

I said forget your past
Don't reply if you're asked
Show me the laughter your sadness conceals,
Let your craziness show
Until you let the hurt go
You'll never know just how good crazy feels.

Everyone's days are numbered
But we're unencumbered
By any promises that we have made,
Stay with me for tonight
I'll make everything right
Let's give in to love's cruel masquerade.

When I woke all that was there
Were my clothes on a chair
She is now at some unknown address,
I knew she had gone
Leaving just before dawn
Wanted freedom more than my love I guess.

She left without leaving a note
But on the mirror she wrote
'Thanks for the love sorry that I cannot stay.'
So I'll never know
Why she had to go
Was it something that I didn't say?

Would I see her again
My blue eyed blond friend
Who loved me with her body and rhyme?
I can only take the chance
And go down to the dance
When the band comes to town the next time.

EARLY TO THE CITY
They know that for them there is no paradise

Those who go down early to the city
Disturb plump rock doves probing the trash,
They go without hope because in their bones
They know for them there is no paradise.

They know that for them there is no love
To shine light into the darkness of their lives,
That light extinguished by their struggle to survive
Buried deep under the burden of their failure.

They are swallowed up by faceless crowds,
Bound around by numbers and irrelevant laws,
Held down by mindless games and futile labours
And the challenges of capricious science.

They are the same people as you and I without the luck,
They took just one too many wrong turns on their road
Finding success and failure were close companions,
Passing strangers are eavesdroppers on their misery.

They walk alone holding their dreams in their arms
Still born dreams soaked through with their tears,
To their backdoor box beds guarded only by the moon
Where they will dream themselves into tomorrow.

If I could open up their hearts and look inside
Hidden there would be my feelings, my dreams,
And if I could look deep enough inside
I'd find their dignity, I'd find their pride.

They who go down early to the city
Rise again at dawn these lost and dispossessed,
And set out once again to take their daily examination
To live another day, to pass the city's test.

LOVE IN STRANGE TIMES
(After 10 weeks in isolation May 2020)

Did I ever think about you?
Did I tell you that I loved you?
Did I ever know your value
Until after I had lost you?

Fears at losing you subsumed now
Into the slogans and the phrases,
They have invented just to stop me
From asking questions that it raises.

Did I ever really want you?
Did I think that I would miss you?
Losing you has made me feel blue,
My world after was smaller too.

Institutions they are all closed now
The temple's comfort has now faltered,
Many lives yet to be sacrificed
On Mammon's million pagan alters.

Are prophesies all coming true?
Is anything that happens new?
The future can't be seen through,
Afterwards we'll all get our due.

I have learnt that I could never share
Saint Bega's pursuit of solitude,
I know now from this experience
We have no point of similitude.

Did I ever want to leave you?
Will I ever again hold you?
Your return's not yet in view,
No moment I don't miss you.

Never before had I imagined
You'd be so cruelly taken from me,
By disciples of democracy
In the efforts made to save me.

Now I know of your true value,
You know I really want you,
You know I really need you,
Freedom you know I love you.

Lines between truth and illusion being redrawn

That is how I will always remember her
Running barefoot through the soft evening rain,
The movement of the silk liquefied her clothes
She is no longer here but that image still remains.

She drifted in unrecognized, silently like mist
Offering no name, holding no invitation,
Merging seamlessly into the general melee
A curious creature of uncertain generation.

She told me she'd let me know about my fortune
Along my palms my lifeline she would trace,
Show me the romance of graveyard ghosts
All inhibitions from my past she would erase.

She said I've been to where you are now headed
I'll take you through the mirror where God plays with sin,
I've known the bliss of dying that is what divides us
Even death can be romantic if you look deep within.

She offered me some comfort in a curtained room
Lines between truth and illusion being redrawn,
I thought I felt love touch me laid there in the gloom
But it slipped right through my fingers and was gone.

Rain formed a light dappled stream upon the path
Falling down like beads of glass off of the trees,
She was standing alone barefoot in the doorway
Arriving without fanfare that's how she would leave.

She ran into the streetlight shimmered rain
The umbrella more for effect than protection,
Never once looking back over her shoulder
No expression of loss in her valediction.

We all die in part for every love we have that's lost
Real or illusory I hunger to see her once again,
She still runs through the back of my memory
Beneath the tunneled trees, barefoot in the rain.

PLAGUE
How futile the fight with ignorance on both sides.

The enemy was invisible our defenses outsmarted
Behind anonymous masks fights had already started,
They recruited from the orphanage and prison as well
And from girls that mean business in the seedy hotel.
Those who never knew innocence those with no name,
All headed up to the front just to keep in the game.

Armies assembled hate concealed in Instagram posts
Sins they'd forgotten marched along with their ghosts,
Advancing toward prejudice, away from compassion
Many joined just because conforming was fashion.
There were so many reasons I couldn't heed their call
Fear, cowardice, indifference I could not list them all.

The local commander had all my movements on tape,
Loyal partisans lined the road to prevent my escape.
Prophets of persuasion with their hands on my wealth
Promised me freedom, said it could be bought off the shelf.
Dealers in delusion said freedom's merely perception
Offering me virtual escape through a dream-filled injection.

Sinking deep into the swamp of the media's inanity
I was retreating slowly into my own insanity.
I headed down to where greedy vultures were feeding
On those seeking asylum with little hope of succeeding.
Money buys freedom when greed and treachery combine
Securing me safe passage through the enemy line.

The enemy first takes out the old letting young ones go past,
They spread the enemy's message, they'll be taken out last.
If you want to be a hero sure I'll tell all of your friends,
But if your friend's now your enemy on whom will you depend?
It's not a good time to be living but a good one for dying,
A good time for the truth but just as good for lying.

Don't look to me for answers, to be honest I don't know
Professors who knew everything have abandoned the show.
While you're heading east to where the battles are won
I will be travelling alone until west of the sun.
I know there's no escape just trying to improve my odds
Against the traitors, false patriots, and the suicide squads.

I hear church bells and wonder if they are ringing for you,
Did you find which side was false and which one was true?
I promised to remember those who stepped into my place,
My conscience betrayed by each forgotten face.
We carry the weight of our past, we'd like to live it again
I wish I didn't know now what I didn't know then.

We find love we thought we had was never ours to own,
The young flowers are all dying before new ones are sown,
Our lives are determined by those who deal out the cards
Some will end up as prisoners, the rest as the guards.
There must be a reason why my life has been spared
Was it that I knew the truth or just that I never cared?

Was the war worth all the agony, would you do it again,
Fighting an intangible enemy to break up the chain?
Be aware what frontiers of ideology you've crossed
You know power shows no mercy to those who have lost.
Will you ever know if you won, the objectives were vague?
There'll be nothing left for losers but the dust of the plague.

TEN ASPIRING WRITERS

They found writing was not as easy as it seems

There were ten aspiring writers
At first everything was fine
One did not understand punctuation,
Notably the apostrophe's location,
So then there were nine.

There were now nine aspiring writers
But one failed to differentiate
Their acronyms from their synonyms,
Their allonyms from their pseudonyms,
So then there were eight.

There were now eight aspiring writers
One developed a syllabic obsession
Their search for a numeric solution
Severely limited their contribution,
So then there were seven.

There were now seven aspiring writers
But one was given to polemics
Chairman ruled it counterproductive
Said this criticism wasn't constructive,
So then there were six.

There were now six aspiring writers
But one of them didn't survive
The pressure of periodic presentation
Which led to the death of inspiration,
So then there were five.

There were now five aspiring writers
But one was shown the door
The pieces they wrote were much too long
And the sexual content much too strong,
So then there were four.

There were now four aspiring writers
One was told his poetry should be free
But for the purposes of timing
He insisted it must be rhyming,
So then there were three.

There were now three aspiring writers
There was him and me and you
They said I used too many clichés, I was cut to the quick,
I could see the writing on the wall, I had to get out quick,
So then there were two.

There were now two aspiring writers
They could see nothing could be done
These writers now were quite bereft
They put their pens in their pockets and left,
And then there were none.

With the writers gone the room was silent
The empty table spoke of shattered dreams,
Empty chairs a testament to their conceit
Their struggles and their ultimate defeat,
They'd found writing was not as easy as it seems.

FRIEND

Your memory sits gently on my heart

Your leaving left a scar across
The landscape of my life
When you changed from someone I know
Into someone who I once knew.

When I lost you I didn't just lose a friend
I lost a part of my identity,
I didn't just lose a person
I lost part of my history.

We lived through each-other's hopes and fears
With love and anger in equal measure.
A million shared experiences
Now I have no one to share them with.

You liked me despite knowing all my secrets
And told me things I wouldn't tell myself,
We knew too much about each-other
To ever consider betrayal.

The world's a lonelier place
When an old friend goes away
They can't be replaced by someone new,
You cannot replace time.

I go whistling past the graveyard
To drown the echo of your voice,
Your memory sits gently on my heart
And leaks out of my eyes in my tears.

You have left a scar that will not heal
It's deep inside me no one else can see.
We promised that we wouldn't grieve
I couldn't keep my part of that deal.

I knew her when she used to rock and roll
When she was everybody's friend,
We searched for love down many roads
Disappointment round every bend.
Living our loneliness every day
We watched each other from afar,
We've had to travel a long, long way
To get to where we are.

We started out on either side
Of a road neither of us knew,
We walked alone for many miles
Using a map neither of us drew.
Not knowing which senses to obey
We let our mind defeat our heart,
We've had to travel a long, long way
To get to where we are.

We found love with our colours fading
It cancelled out all previous pain,
Rescuing us from our shipwrecked lives
We gave each other love then took it back again.
Our memories prevented total decay
After we'd exhausted loves repertoire,
We've had to travel a long, long way
To get to where we are.

Standing now at the end not the beginning
Exhausted by charge and countercharge,
We stand between our attempts at living
Not fooled now by each other's camouflage.
All the worn out wishes we threw away
Now for sale in dream's souvenir bazaar,
Reminders that we traveled a long, long way
To get to where we are.

I knew her when she used to rock and roll
All swinging petticoats and Bardot lips,
I think I loved her right from the start
With her flashing eyes and swaying hips.
The gods made us wait they made us pay
Love wounded us, it left a scar,
Love made us travel a long, long way
To become the lovers that we are.

KEEPING HER DISTANCE

Nothing that we have is ours to keep.

I have a longing now not to be alone,
I am playing back a million memories
Living out the life of my past on my own.
Old photographs provide no remedies
Whilst her whereabouts remains unknown.

I need to be close to her once again
Before my stock of dreams starts running low,
I close my eyes tight to keep her image in
It seeps away in my tears but I cannot let go
Of the pain her fingerprints left on my skin.

My soul is stripped naked by this separation
Losing its light to an all-consuming darkness.
I have no idea of what was her destination,
Left alone with that truth is akin to madness
With no knowledge of distance or duration.

My only certainty is that no help can be found
On the shore where the wave of desolation breaks,
Where even my loudest scream makes no sound.
I am left there to drown in my own mistakes
Among other shipwrecked souls that ran aground.

I thought we were as close as dreams are to sleep
But she slid away from me like hot butter off a knife,
Proving nothing that we have is ours to keep.
Although I let go of love I am holding on to my life
Knowing even a shallow grave would still be too deep.

126

SOLITUDE OF LONGING

The truth filled mirror reminds me I'm alone

Long lost photographs
Exhumed from dusty albums
Form a fistful of lost faces
Which stare out accusingly
Against their long isolation.
I let the memories slip in
Through the gateway of my eyes,
A small stream of the remembered
Flowing across a wilderness
Of the forgotten. Among them
I see her unforgotten face,
My brain turning ventriloquist
To remind me of her voice.

Oh the solitude of longing
And the solitude of loss,
The loss of our belonging
The longing for those lost.

Solitude nourishes the poet
Inspiration born of isolation.
I dance between clichés
To find words worthy of her,
Becoming lost in the
Labyrinth of language.
The truth filled mirror
Reminds me I'm alone.
Childlike I hide myself
In her remembered love,
My failure softened by
The anonymity of
My self-imposed solitude.

Oh the solitude of longing
And the solitude of loss,
The loss of our belonging
The longing for those lost.

CONTEMPLATION
The only time for honesty is when you are alone

He sits looking into the sacred heart of God's gloomy hall
An unbodied crucifix suspended high up on the wall,
He has just the ghosts of his thoughts for company.
The alter is awash with tears which recently were shed
By lovers in their rapture, by the living for the dead.
.

He is leaning over the edge of his finality
Wondering if it was carelessness or stupidity
That lost him all the love he had when he was young.
He is now a seeker out of gloom avoiding the light
Waiting for someone to come and turn on the night.

His lips move, a prayer escapes his unwilling tongue
Merging with haunting echoes of yesterday's evensong.
He's looking for a reason searching heaven for a clue
Finding no answers in each forgiving outstretched limb,
No comfort from those who've walked in the dark like him.

He hears her in whispered prayers of the penitential few
Her fingerprints hanging in the air above the empty pew.
The alter candles are not lit so his sins remain unseen,
Sins held close to his heart wrapped around in sorrow
Living with them today before thinking of tomorrow.

In his head hide the images of everything he's ever seen
And all the things he knows that he will never be.
Cast adrift by fate where his early dreams were grown,
He's still dreaming, but of the past and he always knew
Dreams don't work for everyone even when they're true.

Sat there between the vaulted ceiling and unforgiving stone,
Realising the only time for honesty is when you are alone
But that true solitude in this world is very hard to find.
A man lost in the sterile wasteland of his martyrdom
Despairing at the melancholy figure he'd become.

His love and anger had merged into one in his mind
A contract had been broken which perhaps was never signed.
They told him not to be bitter but he's grown to like the taste,
Knowing there's no difference between the sinner and the saved
And God can shine no light between the foolish and the brave.

The stone-faced saints look down into the near empty space
Reflecting the impenetrable sadness of his face.
Thinking of all things left undone and love's unsated appetite
He wondered if his life had left a trace, had he left his mark
Even if only a glow of phosphorescence in the dark?

These verses are imagined without knowing of his plight
I cannot offer any comfort or his lost love requite
But I see some of his truth in every word I write.
A solitary figure leaves the vaulted space head bowed,
Walking away from love and God to lose himself in the crowd.

OBJECTS
I know their value, I know their cost

I have no object that I treasure
Just the memories in my head
Of all the beauty that I've ever seen
And the things everyone has said.
On the screen inside my mind
I replay all the images from the past,
The happy ones I replay slowly
The ones that hurt me, I play fast.

I do not need an object to remind me
Of those I have loved and those I've lost,
They're held in the archive of my brain
I know their value, I know their cost.
Of all the objects that I've been given
No matter the value they were assigned,
The thing that I have treasured most
Is when they gave to me their time.

Those seeking the illusion of immortality
By passing objects on to their heirs,
Must know in reality they'll all end up
In some forgotten box under the stairs.
But I must admit I have some things
That I haven't yet thrown away,
Maybe it's the finality of the action
That makes me once again delay.

Those letters that she sent me
Hidden in some unopened drawer,
Are just unwanted reminders
Of a love I don't have anymore.
I still wear her wedding ring
For sentimental reasons I suppose,
And I will carry her love within my heart
Until the time that too will decompose.

FAME

Living only inside your reputation

My eyes are staring out to sea
But I'm not looking at the view,
I hope that you are hearing me
I'm reading this for you.

I recall both the time and date
When you said that you'd escape,
And you would have to relocate,
But you'd stay true to me.

I remember when you sang that day
Songs that only you and I could hear,
Dreaming of fame to take you away
From the brooding mills of Lancashire.
Your face was pale like ivory,
Your hair as black as ebony,
Obsidian eyes with false fidelity
Said you'd stay true to me.

In the mirror I see reflections
They are stopping at your face,
Do you still hold the same affections
As that girl who shared my space?
You said fame wouldn't change you
Wouldn't trap and rearrange you,
Distance would not estrange you
That you'd stay true to me.

Back then many promises were made,
Many commitments were implied,
We played out our own masquerade
Where many fantasies have died.
Now I am much more worldly wise
I see through you and your disguise,
See lips tailor-made for lies
Saying you'd stay true to me.

I bought a magazine by chance
Full of provocative pictures of you,
At a festival somewhere in France
With all your reverential crew.
You sported black and gold tattoos
Designed to keep you in the news,
You didn't say in any interviews
That you've stayed true to me.

Standing there on some foreign stage
Your Balmain jeans stuffed full of fame,
A creature of indeterminate age
Cloaked in your non familial name.
Surrounded by praise and adulation
Sustained by recreational medication,
Living only inside your reputation
How could you stay true to me?

I seem to be the unnamed subject
Of many of the songs you write,
Special secrets of young lovers
Sacrificed for your fan's delight.
You are now universally desired
Singing songs our love inspired,
Lines at one time only I admired
Why would you stay true to me?

Now I've found out your location
Communication is forbidden,
Maybe because I have the information
Of where your secrets have been hidden.
Not any part of me it seems
Is allowed to be inside your dreams,
My jealousy doesn't cry, it screams
You should stay true to me.

I don't like this feeling that I'm feeling
Don't know how long that it will last
Don't like what my memory's revealing
I can't seem to let go of the past.
Maybe it's already much too late
To recover from my wounded state,
I know I'll not be healed by hate
If you don't stay true to me.

My letter to you remains unsigned
Maybe true love has made me blind
Because the thought stays in my mind
That you will stay true to me.

I am still here staring out to sea
Tears in my eyes now hide the view,
I hope that you are hearing me
Because I'm reading this to you.

HOPE
All life's absolutes are hidden

Hope is there in the ray of light that
Steals in past the curtains every morning,
In the touch of a lover as the evening light
Fades into the blackness of the night,
In the smile of an innocent child,
In the newly married bride dancing
To the tune of a long remembered song.

I think back to the time when my hope
Was always greater than my despair,
When I just had to reach out my hand
To catch the hope floating in the air,
Now it slips through my fingers like sand.
My dreams do not fit me anymore
And all life's absolutes are hidden.

Hope is beginning to disappear into
The ever receding tide of time.
I'm adrift in the cold ocean of anguish
With the waters closing over my head,
Hands up in surrender, no saving rhyme,
When I feel the grip of a friend and know
I am holding hands with hope.

Although I know the universe itself
Is moving inexorably towards disaster,
And that any love I may encounter
Is a gesture of the ephemeral
Against that which is everlasting.
What will be left to base my life upon
When love leaves me and hope itself is gone?

YOU CAN'T COPYRIGHT LOVE
The best you can do is copyright your own life

Was he in the shadows when we kissed?
Someone in hiding I might have missed?
Maybe her love wasn't mine to hold
But she will always be there crouching
Low in the dark hallways of my mind.

I stand watching the breakers, my pride
Being slowly dissolved in the spindrift.
I walk away down a road paved with
Disintegrating dreams, fenced in by the
Uncaring rain which limits my horizon.

The dying notes of a lone gull's cry
Lays bare the pain and woe of every
Hopeless lover. I had left her reluctantly,
Shuffling with bloodied feet across
The broken glass of my honour.

My thoughts circle like eager vultures
Preying on my wretchedness at losing her.
The love that was stolen from me
Still runs through my every vein,
Her heartbeat still inhabits my shadow.

I did not have the guile to see her mind's
Treason or the courage to taste the sweetness
Of her body. I look forward to the darkness
A blessing of the night, sleep the shortest road
To a more compassionate tomorrow.

Memories of her are now shallower
Than the truth but not as deeply inexact
As a lie. I trample streams of stale tears
Underfoot, they disappear without trace
Into the sterile dust of our history.

Why is it that I could copyright this
Relatively worthless poetry, but it
Proved impossible to protect my love
For her from being plagiarised by some
More skillful but uncaring lover?

Why was I surprised to lose her? Theft is
The common fate of all things rare. The next
Time I won't publish my love but hold it close.
You cannot copyright love or forgiveness,
The best you can do is copyright your own life.

BLAME CULTURE
For all of my many failures the blame is mine alone

I don't seek confirmation
Of my personal point of view,
It is no more or no less valid
Than the one I'd hear from you.

I do not blame my ancestors
For the man that I've become,
I did not have to join their army
Or march to the beat of their drum.

They gave me the colour of my hair
And the colour in my eyes,
They bequeathed to me my gender
And my quite inadequate size.

They offered me no choices
For the colour of my skin
But that's only on the outside
We're all bloody red within.

They offered me their experience
To take any comfort I could find,
They offered me their religion
I looked, but I declined.

They didn't give me my selfishness
They didn't give me my pride
Or the jealousy and anger
That I keep hidden inside.

For all of my many failures
The blame is mine alone,
As for ancestor's actions
I don't condemn them or condone.

Everyone has their own history
All have done something they regret,
Show me a people without blame
Because I haven't found them yet.

Everyone is now searching for
Someone else who they can blame
For their own inadequacies,
For why we can't all be the same.

I have not joined the moral crusaders
Seeking to shame and to condemn,
Not realising the opposing army
Is really just like them.

Some of us are victims of our past,
Some of other people's crimes,
As humans we are imperfect
We are all victims of our time.

What divides us is not our nationality
Our colour, creed or wealth,
It's the jealousy and fear inside your head
Of someone different to yourself.

.

HEROES
A Poem in Ten Syllables

I think I could have become a hero
Rescuing long haired damsels in distress
But my fear of violence and dying
May possibly have hampered my success.

I remember reading epic poems
Of daring deeds played out in times long gone,
Who will poets of today write about
Now all the genuine heroes have gone?

Why aren't they making heroes anymore?
Maybe God has mislaid the hero mould.
Are there no more fair maidens to be saved
No more epic stories to be retold?

Where the noble knight in shining armour
Sat proudly astride his black fiery steed,
Who will ride out alone into the night
To carry out the next heroic deed?

When the storm comes who will be our Noah
And save us all from the impending flood,
Or like Joan be consumed by greedy flame
The price of total commitment to God?

When I am in the heat of the battle
Surrounded by my mortal enemy,
Where will I go to locate a hero
Who will come and stand alongside of me?

The round table, it is unoccupied,
The castle lies in ruins on the hill,
No deeds of honour to be rewarded
No more sacred promises to fulfill.

Each one of our modern superheroes
Are illusions created to deceive,
I require a modern real life hero
To be someone in whom I can believe.

So who will step up to be my hero
To fight for truth and justice in our time?
Although I think I know what is needed
I'm a hero only in my mind.

*(Almost a syllabic ten except the
Last line which I'm afraid has only nine
Which shows I am an anarchic poet
An independent poet for our time)*

GRIEF
My grief will outlast your sympathy

You said I shouldn't be looking so happy
It was too soon, too soon you said,
Too soon after they carried her off
In a slow funeral that left my heart full.

I see the questions behind your eyes
Why aren't I grieving? Where are the tears
That would show you that I cared?
You couldn't know she made me promise
Not to waste time weeping.

I had no words to tell you how much I loved her,
No words to describe the depth of my grief.
Death is a blow that leaves no visible bruises
No amount of tears would bring her back.

What did you want? Aircraft trails in the sky
Telling everyone that she was dead?
For me to see the world only in black and white?
To write poems about the grief inside
That no one really wants to hear?

You who cry too easily at another's loss
Feeling the smart of false tears in your eyes,
Not knowing I wake up broken each morning
And have to force myself back into one piece.

Forty one years under the same roof
Breathing the same air, saying all we
Needed to say with just a look. She held
Her spirit in her name, the only one
To see me without the disguises that I wear.

Why would I waste my tears on you when
My grief will outlast your sympathy?
You aren't there when I go to her in the wood,
That is when I give her my tears.

Love itself is an inevitable invitation to grief,
Living alone now is like a constant suicide.
I am remembering everything that I never said
Knowing every minute I'm alone
I am that minute closer to death.

Now I can only stay here with my hurt,
My grief spilling out in ill measured words
Until the nurse will wipe the last line of
Poetry from my cracked and silent lips.

IS THIS HOW SUCCESS FEELS?
The hopeless futility of man's ambition

He looks out at a steel grey sea,
Loud mouthed gulls scream into the wind
Their cries caught by the curling lip
Of the endless morose waves that slip in
To dissolve with a hiss into the shingle,
Leaving only a darker band washed clean
To show where each spent wave has been.

A shadow races the waves
Towards the shore as a lone cloud
Scuds in from the sea, rain's icy fingers
Destroying any solace that still lingered.
He returns to the sanctuary of his car,
One too expensive for his present need
A reminder of the life he used to lead.

Alone in a town where all is changing,
Where only the street signs stay the same,
Nothing is like it used to be, no use pretending
His world has moved past happy endings.
If only time had allowed him to acclimatise,
He knows the present isn't meant to last
He now only looks forward to the past.

As the daylight drops into the west
He dreams of the village nestled between
The green hills of Gloucestershire
In which he had expected to live and retire,
Where he left his innocence and daydreams
Forsaking safety and family tradition
To search for the rewards of his ambition.

He had secured a lifestyle envied by many
At the expense of family and social life,
Yet wondered if he had spent less of his time
Striving for success and ladders to climb,
He would have realised how often success
Is a deception and not all that it seems
And wouldn't now be wondering what might have been.

Time has moved past him relentlessly
Leaving a space not filled by material reward
Or the hopeless futility of man's ambition.
It is too late now to reverse that position,
He's left with only those friends and lovers hidden in his heart.
He knows that he could have given more and taken less
Thinking now that survival is his only real success.

OXYGEN IS LIFE
Nothing really matters, it's only death that counts
(Amid the COVID-19 pandemic 2020)

She stood before him, his humanity was hanging by a thread
I never knew 'till now how much I wanted you, he said.
I have taken you for granted, never given you much thought,
I really need you now to fight this infection I have caught.
I didn't know how much I loved you until you were almost lost
Now I'd give anything to keep you, no matter what the cost.

She said, why do you think I should give you anything you ask?
He thought he saw her smile from behind her paper mask,
He said, please forgive me for all the wrongs that I have done
I'm not asking you for much, just a little oxygen.

He was making his final stand from inside a plastic bubble tent
Not sure that she had understood the message that he'd sent,
He wanted to tell her he'd have loved her more if only he had known
How easy it was to lose her and how quickly she'd be gone.

He tried to raise himself as he slid into the darkness of her heart
Reaching out for her hand as she made ready to depart,
At last she relented, gave him her sweetest air, he breathed it in
She dragged him back towards the light from the quagmire of his sin.

Having nearly lost her, having nearly let her slip away
He did not think he could love her more than he did that day.
He has reassessed his values, all previous priorities renounced
Realising nothing really matters, it's only death that counts.

GIVING UP ON YOU
I wrote them all for you

Every word I've written
I wrote them all for you,
You are there in all my dreams
And in everything I do.
Words used in each imperfect line
I believed them to be true,
When in the forest of suspicion
I used them to get us through.
Is it too late for me to say that I'm sorry
Or to turn back time and rewrite our story?

Every song I have ever written
You were there in every note,
You were hiding in every sound
Escaping from my throat.
My love was there disguised
In every line I wrote,
For any hurt I caused you
My words are the antidote.
Satan is laughing because I let your love go by,
The tears of crying angels are falling from the sky.

When I was writing in darkness
You bathed me in your light,
Found me when I tried to hide
In the shadows of the night.
You were the provocation behind
Any words born out of spite,
When you appealed for peace
I was still up for the fight.
If we were just actors performing on a stage,
I would take back the script and tear out that page.

Now everything I write about you
I have to write in the past tense,
It took me many years to cross
The lines of your defence.
You are questioning my honesty
But I write from experience,
You claim if any of it is true
That it's just coincidence.
You said I had betrayed you, I told you I had not,
You said 'Not with your body you betrayed me in your thought.'

Every word I have ever written
I wrote them all for you,
I thought you'd found what I had lost
But you'd found my secrets too.
You held me close through winter
In spring you disappeared from view,
I can't believe I'm writing
That I've given up on you.
My first words were dreams we had right at the start,
These last tears of blood torn straight out of my heart.

THE STALKER
Then I will be free

He is always there beside me, always in my sight
Except in the privacy of night.
He knows my every movement, there is no escape,
Following my footsteps
Whenever I'm awake.
I must be careful about what I let him see
He's always watching me,
He's always watching me.

Dressed in black or grey, the most obvious of spies
Never wearing a disguise,
Not answering any questions that I pose
If he understands me
It never shows.
He can hear me talking, that's why I'm whispering
In case he listens in,
In case he listens in.

He can change his shape it seems just on a whim
Sometimes fat, sometimes slim.
In the sunlight he's dark and menacing
In the gloom he's pale
And self-effacing.
I don't trust this amorphous ever-changing entity
Sharing my identity,
Sharing my identity.

He has seen all of my triumphs and all my failures too
He sees everything I do.
He is a co-conspirator in all of my many sins
He appears with the light
As each new day begins.
I don't know if he's friendly, I don't know him well
How can I really tell?
How can I really tell?

He lurks behind me where the sunlight's dim
Until the dark devours him.
He is just a nameless, sad and lonely creature
He's like me but part erased
An outline with no features.
His present and his future actions are already cast
He's following my past,
He's following my past.

No one can really tell you what your shadow's for
Spread-eagled on the floor,
A malevolent presence silent and morose
Never wanting to be held
But always staying close.
Clothed in oak, they'll close my eyes so I can't see
Then I will be free,
Then I will be free.

IS THAT WHAT YOU WANTED?
The only things I believe in are those I left behind

You captured my soul
You held it to ransom,
You held the lock's combination
Warned me the numbers were random.

I made you a crown from my words
And a ring from my silence,
Thought that was what you wanted
For me to show my repentance.

I hear the echo of your voice
From the first time that we met,
Blown backwards toward me
From the lips of my regret.

I thought I'd left the ashes
Of our love far behind me,
I have travelled a long way
Just so you wouldn't find me.

While we've been apart
A million dreams have come true,
As I know none were mine
They must have all been for you.

When I woke up to the truth
I was back with the blind,
The only things I believe in
Are those I left behind.

Now every path turns towards you
Every tunnel is haunted,
You know I cannot escape
Is that what you wanted?

THINKING ALOUD
This is all part of life's song to you

The notes you hear brought to you on the wind
The rhythm of raindrops on the leaves,
The sound of waves breaking on the shore
The cry of gulls borne on the summer breeze,
This is all part of life's song to you
It's there to put your tormented soul at ease.

The rippling of a stream across the stones
Mist rising in the morning heat,
The swoosh of snow slumping off a tree
Ice crystals crackling beneath your feet,
This is all part of life's song to you
It's there to take down some of your conceit.

The laughter of children as they play
The ring of bells drifting to you from afar,
The sound of choristers at evensong
The hum of the engine of an unseen car,
This is all part of life's song to you
It's there to make peace with who you are.

The voices of lovers who are long since gone
That seep unwanted through the shroud,
Are there to remind you of what might have been,
Like the rumble of thunder from a far off cloud.
This is all part of life's song to you
It's just the sound of nature thinking aloud.

MOVING ON

We have both learnt not to look for perfection.

I can tell you've already moved on
You kissed me like you'd never been my lover,
Your eyes show our boundaries redrawn
Your lips tell me the great affair is over.

You tried to find the love we had before
Firing love tipped arrows towards my mind,
None reached the target you were aiming for
Like your love the archers were blind.

You moved on but where were you going
Did you return to the places we used to know,
To where the sea like our love was unrolling
Only to be drowned in the undertow?

Although time by its very nature moves on
Our love somehow became lost in the past,
If time had stood still maybe we could have won
Only the future can say how long love will last.

For me and for you there would be no way back
We had both moved on in a different direction,
Knowing now love is never pure white or jet black
We have both learnt not to look for perfection.

JUNKYARD

I am falling upward from my past

So that was her. It probably cost a lot to look that cheap.
She had been on the losing side of too many wars,
The girl I had been looking for on and off for years
Now a bow fronted old woman with dusty drawers.

I remembered her as on the pretty side of beautiful
Imperfect memory acting as growing old's veneer,
I knew I too wouldn't be the man that she remembered
Our heads retain images captured when eyes were clear.

In my youth I confused passion and beauty with love
Experience showed me not every lover is sincere,
I then looked for love not in my eye but in my heart
I wanted more than another heartache souvenir.

I elbowed my way past fragments of previous heartbreaks,
Rummaged through a clutter of half-forgotten romances
Hoping to stumble across a jewel among the junk,
A melancholy search not giving much for my chances.

She started off as a one night stand that wouldn't let go
Her passion hitting me so hard that I forgot to breathe,
But above that vulgar flight of craving and low desire
Love unfolded that was deeper than the lust beneath.

A girl with skin so delicate it was almost opaque
As if the full moon was orbiting inside her skin,
She was a flower before any hand had touched it
An Aconitum, beauty masking poison held within.

On the surface a perfectly presented penthouse
Life was all about her, she always dressed the part,
I did not see the slum hiding inside of her
Our love soon too lost to save, too cold to restart.

The life of this affair was as short as it was hot,
Her behaviour nine parts eagle only one part dove.
She said I betrayed her but I had just become myself
Rendered helpless, buried under an avalanche of love.

When she left she broke many things I could not repair
I know she told me lies but I believed her none the less,
She was the only treasure in my collection of junk
I hoped she would return, I had given her my address.

She left me with nothing not even with a smile
Consigning me to the bleak graveyard of her passion,
With the friendless bodies of other unburied lovers
The common fate of all love without compassion.

The main enemy of love is maybe life itself
I had wasted those years taunted by her memory,
Her sad reality let me see my past with clearer eyes
It hurt to realise my first love had been delusory.

Today I am just a body that is trapped within the truth
Age corrupts the beauty memory and time will flatter,
Love was the only relevance when we were in our youth
Outside lay the junkyard of our lives which didn't matter.

Now I'm back out in the junkyard looking for a treasure
Regretting my obsession and the wasted time that's passed,
My failures rest in endless piles inside an aging head
I live through them all again falling upward from my past.

SIGNALS

I was looking for love, she more for sin.

She stood apart from all the others
Between the music and the wine,
The road behind littered with those
Who had misinterpreted her signs.
Oh yes you were the pretty one
You were every young man's dream.
They were waiting patiently in line
For your signal to turn green.

They came to you in innocence
The uncrowned dancehall queen,
You left so many without their pride
All those that fell down in between
Their desire and your indifference
Into the broken hearts machine,
Their love disintegrating
Before your signal turned to green.

We came closest when our shadows met
I was looking for love, she more for sin,
I wanted it deeper but couldn't finish
What my mind had pencilled in.
She did nothing to put me at my ease
She had me begging on my knees
Whatever colour I thought I'd seen
I knew her signal was not on green.

Love's signals are not absolute
They depend on your level of conceit,
All the other dance hall failures
Returned my wan smile of defeat.
As morning light gained on the gloom
It was a lesson learned, never assume
Desire alone can secure your dream,
When you move, be sure her signal's green.

TOO DERELICT TO MODERNISE
Can't do freedom, I Need rules

Writing a poem with
No rhyme is difficult.
I fight off my hidden rhymester.
Must avoid Iambic pentameters.
Is prose poetry?
Question too hard.
Free verse then?
Write anything no rules
Seems crazy
But many poets do it.
No superfluity.
Are all my words necessary?
I cut out half the words
Remember show don't tell.
Show don't tell
For God's sake,
Now I've got even
More bloody words.

Feeling old,
Can't do freedom,
I Need rules.
Still running on steam
Must electrify.
Too old for conversion.
Pipes plugged,
Cogs corroded,
Neurons knackered.
Old. Too damn old.

I just can't get this free verse right,
Although at one stage I thought I might,
Thought I'd written something that was free
But looked again and I could see
What I'd written, which I thought was deep,
Wasn't free just very cheap.
Every time I tried to improve my verse
Whatever I did just made it worse,
I tried a stream of consciousness
But that result failed to impress,
I tried to show and not to tell
But that approach didn't go too well.
I tried brevity but in my defense
When I cut out words it made no sense.
Creativity was lost without my rhymes
Although I tried it many times,
I found the dreaded rhymesters curse
Drove me back towards close metered verse.

Tried to write free verse never found the trick,
Maybe I'm a Luddite maybe just thick!
I've realised poets in my situation
Are just too derelict for modernization.

LIVING IS NOT EASY

The world's lost all respect for misery.

Years ago life was so easy
The seas were blue, the fields were green,
We obeyed teachers and our parents,
We stood in silence for the Queen.
Now we respect celebrities
Desire many things we do not need,
Lives lived only on the surface
Driven by envy and by greed.

Hypocrisy is the new truth
Fame is the new religion,
To achieve ignorance appears to be
The height of our ambition.
I am told that the end is coming
For the life we have come to know,
Due to our selfish profligacy
Travelling fast instead of slow.

They say we must change our lifestyle
Less resources must be consumed,
Not telling us it's not the planet
But only humans that are doomed.
While we are trying to save the world
Saving ourselves seems improbable,
Our desire for more possessions
Would appear to be unstoppable.

Happiness used to be a sometime state
It now appears to be compulsory,
In our frantic pursuit of pleasure
The world's lost all respect for misery.
If I said now life was simpler
Than before, I would be lying,
Living to me is so obviously
Much more difficult than dying.

THE BOOKKEEPER

To find the secrets only dead men know.

I've travelled across an ocean of unused words,
Climbed over the high walls of my pride,
Pushed through a forest of rejections
Only to find her on the other side.

She was the custodian of every written word
Who looked upon all writers with disdain,
An old and haggard keeper of the books
Her bony hand recording each author's name.

All the poetry of misery and death she memorized
Work of those lost to suicide stored in secret files,
The poetry of beauty going unrecognized
As she moved silently up and down the aisles.

Her piercing eyes scanned the pages in my head
Of an imagined book I had yet to write,
And without pause she printed a rejection slip
Giving me no chance to put things right.

She said my worst was better than my best
Too many of the lines I used were borrowed,
That my work left her deeply unimpressed
It wouldn't even be a memory tomorrow.

The crone shuffled silently toward me
Like the Grim Reaper arriving at Halloween,
Escorting me through the door marked failure
That had swallowed up a million dreams.

She followed me out then told me,
I'd be held so that I could learn
To write verses that she approved of
Before I was allowed to return.

She said for every pleasure a writer feels
They have to take equivalent pain,
They must lose some part of their self
For every single line they gain.

Saying all the words I'd written were recorded
And they would all count against me now,
I'd be given time to put them in the right order
But she was not going to tell me how.

I was being held there against my will
The doors locked and the windows barred,
She thought a mere poet would never escape
Not knowing I'd made friends with the guard.

I paid the guard off with a Sonnet
Cries of the damned were released in his smile,
I was a poet I needed the freedom
To write lines in my own imperfect style.

I wanted to leave the madness of trying
To be someone I was never meant to be,
And see nature again with clearer eyes
And write about the beauty of just being free.

To walk the shore that no ship has ever seen
Where the full moon is licking up the sea,
Where waves send hissing tongues into the sand
Safe from prevailing injustices that wait for me.

I'm going to a place a thousand miles away
From where every book ever written is stowed,
To discover the words those old poets used
To try and find the secrets only dead men know.

BELIEF

He'd sell his soul for a Bond Girl's kiss

I need to see the proof
Before I can believe,
They're demanding repentance
Before I'm reprieved.

The priest is telling me
My soul is already lost,
But not on which side of the grave
I'll be paying the cost.

Although I know I'm the leader
Of the state that I am in,
They say if I just go to church
I can dump all of my sin.

I've never believed in some
Predetermined destiny,
I'm just hanging from a branch
Of my family tree.

Don't think I'll get into heaven
I'm carrying too much sin,
If I make it to the gates
I'll need a gun to get in.

They say I'd sell my soul
For a Bond Girl's kiss,
I'd say that's a pretty good deal
If you're an atheist.

I don't think it matters
Which road I take,
I will be defined by the ashes
I leave in my wake.

TIME IS MY ENEMY
My future is irresistibly closing in

When I look in front of me
I see that too few years remain.
The time I've had is now inside of me
With all the sin that time contains,
And all the dreams that now will never be.

I see empty chairs of friends who've gone away
A few are still close, most cannot be found.
I see spaces left by things I didn't say,
Hearing silence where once was sound.
I can't see far from where I am today.

When I look in front of me
And squint my eyes until they hurt,
I think it is her image I can almost see
As heartless memory my eyes subvert,
But I know the past is truth so it cannot be.

I can't retrieve the tears I cried,
Or buy back love I gave away for free.
It's too late a new direction to decide
I am close to where I have to be,
I can almost see the other side.

When I look in front of me
My future is irresistibly closing in
My past ever more difficult to see.
No time left for new ventures to begin,
My destination is no longer up to me.

FROM WHERE I STAND
Everything I have is the fruit of my own labour

Why are you asking me to move from my position
Where walls define my view and muffle sound?
I am not seeking paradise, I do not fear perdition
I am happy to shelter here on lower ground.

I never saw it as my duty to change society at large
Or bring equality to everyone across the land,
Rather I sought to avoid society's many failings
And simply find a safe place in which to stand.

I have heard about the homeless and dispossessed
The underprivileged, the forsaken and the damned,
Although I've been made aware of their existence
I can't see them from the place in which I stand.

.

I have never sought a place with the disciples
I hide among the million hearts they don't command,
Samaritan's voices begging for my charity
Cannot be heard from the place in which I stand.

Everything I have is the fruit of my own labour
I asked for no favours, I made no demands,
I inherited nothing but my name and my shadow
I have no regrets about where I chose to stand.

You tell me it's time to leave my cloistered avenue,
Time for me to move and stand on higher ground
Where everyone's in view, no suffering hidden,
In a place where a conscience may be found.

LAST OF THE LINE
A life of repeats isn't for me

I am the last of the line
There will be no more after me,
I have no sons or brothers to carry my name
When I die, we will just cease to be.

I am the last of the line
When young I never gave it a thought,
Now I am older I think it's a loss to the world
Then again .... maybe it's not.

I am the last of the line
As a result of inadequate conception,
I produced no progeny of either sex
But extinction was not my intention.

I am the last of the line
My exceptional genes will be lost,
Pain from lack of descendants is softened
By how much I have saved on the cost.

I am the last of the line
No one will search my family tree,
If my name appears as some distant relative
They won't have been searching for me.

I am the last of the line
I never desired immortality,
I have experienced most of what life can offer
A life of repeats isn't for me.

I am the last of the line
I do not yearn to be remembered,
My name will be finally used at my funeral
When into ashes I will be rendered.

I am the last of the line
Although friends may at first reminisce,
In time I'll disappear from their thoughts
And I'll no longer be missed.

I am the last of the line
No marble slab will my name wear,
I'll be scattered wide in Owlet Wood
Only she will know that I am there.

I am the last of the line
I will leave nothing behind me of note,
Just a book sold on an internet web site
Containing some verses what I have wrote.

"If you're reading this...

Congratulations, you're alive.
If that's not something to
smile about, then I
don't know
what is."

Chad Sugg

Printed in Poland
by Amazon Fulfillment
Poland Sp. z o.o., Wrocław

61858264R00099